To Hilda

THE LOOK

Paris for the Last Time

God Bless!

MARIA PRYOR HERNDON

Maria

ARCHWAY PUBLISHING

Copyright © 2020 Maria Pryor Herndon.

All rights reserved. No part of this book may be used or reproduced by any means, graphic, electronic, or mechanical, including photocopying, recording, taping or by any information storage retrieval system without the written permission of the author except in the case of brief quotations embodied in critical articles and reviews.

This is a work of fiction. All of the characters, names, incidents, organizations, and dialogue in this novel are either the products of the author's imagination or are used fictitiously.

Archway Publishing books may be ordered through booksellers or by contacting:

Archway Publishing
1663 Liberty Drive
Bloomington, IN 47403
www.archwaypublishing.com
1 (888) 242-5904

Because of the dynamic nature of the Internet, any web addresses or links contained in this book may have changed since publication and may no longer be valid. The views expressed in this work are solely those of the author and do not necessarily reflect the views of the publisher, and the publisher hereby disclaims any responsibility for them.

Any people depicted in stock imagery provided by Getty Images are models, and such images are being used for illustrative purposes only. Certain stock imagery © Getty Images.

ISBN: 978-1-4808-8621-6 (sc)
ISBN: 978-1-4808-8622-3 (e)

Library of Congress Control Number: 2019920524

Print information available on the last page.

Archway Publishing rev. date: 07/09/2020

Dedication:

To Bill:

A model of a man;
    a veteran,
        a teacher,
            a Christian,
                and a distant friend,

and to The Late Bernard and Jackie Origet, who loved each other until the end, and who continued to open their home to me whenever I was able to scrounge up the airfare to Paris. Also to Anny and Jean Rene' Talopp who helped me with my French studies, Jean-Bernard Origet who loved to sing Rock and Roll, Catherine who taught me to climb the rocks of Fontainbleau, and finally, Serge (her husband) who taught me how to roast a duck.

"The Look"
By Sara Teasdale

Strephon kissed me in the spring,
Robin in the fall,
But Colin only looked at me
And never kissed at all.

Strephon's kiss was lost in jest,
Robin's lost in play,
But the kiss in Colin's eyes
Haunts me night and day.

(The poem is in public domain.)

CHAPTER ONE

MELISSA HAD FALLEN in love with Bill at Chicago Teachers College. It hadn't been her intention. She had been there to get an education, get a teaching credential, graduate, and get a job at a good school. She had been tired of being poor, tired of having clothes that hadn't fit, and shoes that had hurt her feet. She hadn't even had much of a chance to make friends. She had been commuting home to school, and when school had been out, she had always gone home to study alone.

The sense of being watched had come suddenly, in the beginning of her final semester. She had started having the feeling whenever she had been at her locker. It hadn't been a feeling that had frightened her, just an awareness that someone was watching her.

After several days, when she had felt that she couldn't stand it any longer, she'd stepped back from her locker into the hallway to look in both directions. But, since she hadn't seen anyone looking in her direction, she had decided that perhaps she'd been mistaken.

However, the next day, when she had gone to her locker, the feeling had resurfaced. She had felt someone's eyes on her again. Hoping to end this "game", she'd decided to stay at her locker a little longer each time that she was there. She had also started up conversations with the students who'd had lockers next to hers; when finally, she had caught a glimpse of a young man in black who seemed to be watching her.

He'd been an attractive young man. He'd had on clothes that, she had been certain, would have fit no one else. His shoes had been highly polished and his slacks had been pressed and creased. His jacket had been black leather, and had fit him like a second skin. You didn't call a man "stunning", but she had been stunned and awestruck by how handsome he was!

She hadn't been able to believe that he had been watching her! He had been too gorgeous! So, she had convinced herself that she had been mistaken and that thought had made her less nervous. She had also convinced herself that perhaps he had only seemed to be looking at her, when he had probably only been looking in her direction. Being too nervous to walk near him, she had closed her locker and gone in the opposite direction. However, that decision had made her late to her next class.

When she had entered the classroom, all of the seats had been filled except for one in the front. She had slipped as quietly as she could into that one, but she soon felt that same feeling that she had felt at her locker. He must have been there, but she hadn't dared to turn around!

The next day, when she'd gone to her locker, the feeling had been gone! She had been disappointed, but admittedly relieved. As she had headed off to class, and was descending the wide staircase in the middle of the building, she suddenly saw him! He was standing in the corner of the landing! His arms were crossed, and it was obvious to her that he had placed himself there so that she could not help but see him. His eyes had met hers; he hadn't smiled, and his look had been intense. In a panic, she had accelerated her descent, and had nearly run! Once in class, she again sat in the front, unable to turn around and look for him, but certain that he was there. She'd felt his presence! Her heart had been pounding so strongly that, she had been sure that the people sitting next to her could hear it! She had sat there dazed and trembling, unable to hear or take notes during the lecture.

When class had been dismissed, she had felt her heart still pounding to the point that she thought she would faint! She had stood and slowly turned to leave, but she'd had to sit back down. She had taken several deep breaths as she had scanned the room and had seen that everyone had left. However, it had struck her that he might be waiting outside! So, she'd taken a few more minutes to gather her things and more deep breaths before she was ready to enter the hallway. Rising a second time, she had slowly walked to the door. When she had entered the hallway, it had been empty. She'd released a a heavy sigh, and realized that she was feeling somewhat relieved, but also very disappointed. So, she had headed out of the building, not even bothering to go to her locker.

She hadn't known how much longer she would be able stand this! She'd wondered why he wouldn't speak to her? She's wondered what he had wanted from her? Waiting for him to do so had been torturous! She was sure that if he didn't do, or say something soon, she would have a heart attack! No one had ever looked at her the way he had on the landing. No one that handsome had ever even noticed her.

She had always been a little shy, and definitely not very popular. She had to know what he wanted from her! So, the following day, she had come to school earlier than usual so that she could stand down the hall near the classroom until she had seen that he had entered. Then she had walked to the doorway, heart pounding, where she stood briefly, in order to see where he had sat. She had scanned the room and had seen him sitting in the back row! After taking several deep breaths, she had decided that she would sit next to him! The seat was vacant, and it had seemed to be the only way to end this nerve-wracking game.

With all of the courage she could muster, she had excused herself to everyone she moved past to sit in that vacant seat next to him. She hadn't been able to look at his face, but she couldn't help but notice his hand resting on his thigh. Wow! Was all she was able to think. His hand had been firm and strong looking, his thigh muscular. When she slid into the seat, she had looked at his profile.

"Hi." She had whispered as she sat down. He hadn't turned to look at her, but she saw a smile slowly form on his lips.

"Hi." He had responded quietly, then, at last, he had turned to look at her, to look in her eyes, and there it was "the look"; intense, kind, soft, dark, teasing, warm, and desiring. It had taken her breath away!

"My name is Bill." He had whispered. Then he had turned back to listen to the lecture.

Now, over 30 years later, she was still in love with Bill. After they had gotten to know each other, he had told her that he was engaged. He had told her that he had had no choice; that he had to marry someone he had known since childhood. He had explained that his family had expected it. However, he had also made it clear that he thought that he loved her too and hadn't wanted to hurt her, his fiancé or his family. To complicate matters, even more, he had enlisted in the military and had to go serve immediately after graduation. She had learned that she was fourth, behind fiance', family and the military.

On the final day of classes, they had taken the same bus and had gotten off at the fountain where she'd had to transfer. There was to be no "good-bye kiss", not even a hug. In fact, she had been glad that he had made no effort to touch her. If he had, she would have held on to him, and would not have been able to let go. She had been devastated, hurt to the point that her heart ached, but she had held her feelings inside.

"Good-bye." He had whispered, softly, sadly.

"Good-bye." She had said as she had turned and walked away swiftly, trying to hold back her tears. She had never looked back. She had left him sitting in front of the fountain on 51st and Drexel Blvd.; his head had been bowed, and his shoulders had been slumped.

On graduation day, she had made no effort to find him. Instead of being jubilant, she had felt indescribably sad. It had been like she had been in a fog. She had gone through the motions. She had smiled and said "good-bye" to her classmates. She had hugged her parents and had smiled brightly, but her heart had been broken. If a person's soul could be broken, then she had felt that he had broken hers.

Years later, she had seen him coming out of a grocery store in which she had been shopping. He had been standing out front talking to two small children. Her heart had leaped in her chest, and she had wanted so desperately to hug him, to hold on to him one last time. He had seemed taller, and a little weary, but he had looked at her like he always had. She had wondered how he could have hurt her so!

How dare he reappear out of nowhere looking as handsome as ever! She had thought while standing away from him. "Are these your children?" She had asked looking at the two little boys that were with him.

"Just this one." He said softly, pointing to one of them.

"How do you do?" She had said, bending down and reaching to shake the little boy's hand.

"Okay." The little boy had said softly, looking up at her.

It had been an awkward moment, but it had been etched in her memory. She had been sure that it would be the last time she would ever see Bill. She had moved away and had only been in Chicago to visit her sister. It had been just a coincidence that she had run into him at this grocery. The kids had been fidgeting while they had stood looking at each other. It had probably felt like forever to them, but to her, it had not been long enough.

"Well, it was great seeing you again!" Melissa had said. She had felt the tears welling up in her eyes. So, though she had longed to spend as much time as she could with him, she knew she couldn't.

"You look great!" Bill had said softly. Then he had added, "take care of yourself."

Once again, she had been the one who had turned and walked away. She hadn't looked back. She couldn't look back.

Twenty or so years after that, she had connected with him on e-mail. When she had asked him how he was, he had responded that he was well; however, he had made a point of letting her know that he was divorced. He also had added that he "vaguely remembered a very sweet young woman from college". Melissa had been hurt to know that he hardly remembered her. You would have thought that that would have discouraged her, but she couldn't help hoping that finally, they might get together, until that final sentence. He had ended the e-mail with "I am seeing someone."

Melissa had gone into a slight depression. He had "put the nail in the coffin", and as always, when life kicked her in the gut, she thought of her mother who had always reminded her that "what's for you, you will get!" Though she seemed to never be able to forget Bill, she vowed to try to do so. But, no matter how hard she tried, she couldn't. He had been her first real love. The memories were like a sore that though it had healed, the scar remained and continually reminded her of what might have been.

CHAPTER TWO

SHE COULDN'T LIVE in the same town, knowing Bill, was also there. So, she had moved as far away as she could get; she had moved to California. No one knew about him, not her parents, not her sister, no one. She had found it painful to think about him, let alone talk about him. She had put her yearbook on a top shelf, out of her way. She still couldn't even look at his picture without tears welling up in her eyes, and since that was the only reason she had bought the yearbook; she hoped that by not looking at him she would forget him.

She had tried to marry. She had tried twice, but she hadn't been very good at it. Her first marriage had only lasted long enough to convince her that she had made a very bad mistake! The only good thing that had come out of it had been her son, Joseph. She had waited seven years to marry again. She had done so because everyone had kept telling her that her son needed a father. Well, that marriage had been even worse than her first! Her first husband had abused himself, with drugs, and her second husband had abused both her first son and his own son. So, when she couldn't stand it any longer, she had filed for legal separation. Her second husband had been so angry that he counter-filed for divorce. That had been fine with her! She had really wanted a divorce, but she had been reminded over and over again that

Christians should not divorce, except for reasons of abandonment or adultery, neither of which had he committed.

She had been divorced a long time, and she had taught French for a long time, so she had decided to take a final trip back to Paris. She called it "her farewell tour!" She had arranged a stop-over in Chicago, so that she could visit her sister. However, she knew that this time there would be no chance encounter with Bill, no accidental meeting. She would not be leaving the airport; her sister would meet her there. She had booked a room at a nearby hotel for one night, so they could spend the evening together having dinner, talking, and maybe watching a movie. But, just like she had done the first time, she was going to France alone. No one would miss her, except maybe her sons and her grandchildren; however, she knew that they would be okay with her being gone for a month or so.

She hadn't really made any concrete plans. She knew that she could do whatever she wanted. This time, she would not be leading a tour. Maybe she would take another language course at The Sorbonne, or The Language School (Alliance Francaise). She had done that the first time, and she had been surprised and pleased that she had placed in the 3rd level class, out of 5, for "foreigners". Or, perhaps she would just be a tourist and not make any real plans.

Melissa had loved French ever since she had been 14 years old. That had been when she had taken her first French class in high school. She had loved the way it sounded, its cadence and rhythm. Her first French teacher had made it sound like German and had made conjugation of verbs the main focus of the class, but thankfully there had been a language lab where students could listen to French so they could develop and practice their accents.

She had loved all of her high school French teachers, except for Monsieur Bien-Aime'. It made her laugh to remember that "bien aime' " means "beloved", when he had been the most unpleasant.

He had never seemed pleased with anything she did. He was the only one to give her a C.

In college, she had had Daniel Boehme, whom she had learned to adore. He had been young and very delicate looking. One might go so far as to say that he looked "sickly". He had been extremely pale. To Melissa, his skin had looked translucent. His hair had been soft and light brown. His eyes had been large and very blue. In fact, he had looked more like a child than a college professor. He had been the best! One afternoon towards the end of the semester Mr. Boehme had approached her quietly and had handed her Final to her. Out of a possible 250 points, she had received 232. No one had ever scored 100% on Prof. Boheme's tests because they were tough. They had included dictation, translation, vocabulary, grammar, and spelling. When he graded the exams, he graded every little thing. Needless to say, Melissa had been proud to have earned an A even though her paper hadn't been perfect. While she was reviewing her paper; he paused at her desk and said quietly that she was one of the best students that he had ever had and that she must go to Paris to become more proficient.

She was 19 years old, living at home, and she had never spent the night away from home, except at her best friend's house. But, because of his encouragement, she made plans to visit Paris. She had decided to take the next semester off. She had talked her best friend, into going as well, but on the day that they were to buy their tickets; her friend had told her that she had thought that she had been "joking around", and that she hadn't the money and couldn't go. So, with the encouragement of her mother, Melissa had purchased her ticket and had gone alone. She had saved up enough money to go to Paris for one semester. However, what she hadn't done is book a place to stay. She had stupidly decided that she would find a room once she had arrived. It had been a dumb idea!

She had flown out of O'Hare Airport on a "red-eye". It

had been a beautiful flight! As the plane had flown Northeast, towards the North Pole. The sky colors had gone from black to purple, to red, to orange, to yellow to snowy white. She had never seen anything like it! She had taken a plane by a company called Icelandic. There had been one stop-over, and it had been in some place that she had never heard of: "Reykjavik, Iceland". A fairly long layover had been announced, with a short tour of the island; however, she had been so nervous, that she had chosen to sit in the airport until time to board. All that she remembered was that it had been cold and damp. She had almost been tempted to buy a very warm wool sweater that she had seen in the airport gift shop. But not knowing how much she would be spending in Paris, she resisted.

Crossing the Atlantic had terrified her so much, that she had decided to try to sleep. She hadn't dared to even look out of the window. She had awakened when she heard the stewardess announce that they were about to descend and to fasten all seatbelts. When she exited the airplane, it had finally hit her where she was, and how far away from home she was. However, she didn't panic, and that had amazed her!

She had hailed a taxi, and asked the driver, in French, if he knew where she could find a room for the night. He had said he did, and after a short ride he had stopped in front of a small hotel. Having never been to Paris before, she hadn't known whether or not the hotel was in a "good part of town", but she had liked the looks of it so she had registered.

The concierge had been very nice. Melissa had been given a small room with a view of the street, and a bathroom that had to be shared. When she had entered her room, she realized how exhausted she was! She had put her suitcase on a chair, and without undressing, she had lain across the bed and had gone immediately to sleep.

It was when she had awakened that she had panicked! She

hadn't gone out for 3 days! She had found that the French that she was hearing was too fast! The only thing that had prompted her to leave the room was the concierge. She had whispered through the door and had asked;

"Qu'as-tu?" ("What's wrong?")

"Je vais bien, mais j'ai peur!" (I'm fine, but I am afraid.!) Melissa had responded. She had gone on to explain that she had just realized that she didn't know anyone in Paris, that she was afraid to go out, that she was 7,000 miles from home, and that she had never been that far from home before!

The concierge had responded simply by saying, "Ah, mais c'est Paris!" (But, It's Paris!)

Having been able to converse with the concierge had encouraged her, so she had ventured down to breakfast. After having eaten a croissant and having drunk a café' au lait, she had asked for directions to L'Alliance Francaise, and which bus she should take. Then she had put on her trench coat, and ventured out; and as they say, "the rest is history!'

Through a small miracle, she had met a family that adopted her, and who's teenage children had taken it upon themselves to help her with her French.

So, her nervousness had soon turned to excitement; as each day, she had gained more confidence, and very soon, she had begun to feel like a native. Melissa smiled as she remembered that first experience. When she returned to college, she had looked for Professor Boheme, to thank him, but sadly, he had transferred to another college. Regrettably, she had never been able to tell him how grateful she had been for his encouragement.

Now, settling into her seat on the plane, she closed her eyes and nodded off. She had never been a good flier. Her nerves were always on edge until that first bump on the landing runway. However, this time she was able to relax a little. She had prayed for God's protection, so she knew she was in His hands. She thought of her grandchildren and sons. Though she would miss them, she knew that if something were to happen to her, they would grieve, yet get on fine. They were grown and quite independent. Though she had been the one to take them to church, the one who had read them Bible stories, the one who had led them to accept Christ, the one who had tried to instill in their hearts what her mother had always said to her, when she had seen someone less fortunate; "there but for the grace of God go I." She felt at peace. She had left them an old insurance policy. They wouldn't be rich when she passed on, but they would at least have a home and a little money for the grandchildren for college.

Paris! She thought about visiting some of the other cities in France. She had been to Nantes before for a month or so. It was like a little Paris. It had been nice, but it was pretty much known for its beach, and she had never been a beach person. The family that she had stayed with had passed on, so she no longer knew anyone there. She had also been to Fountainbleau for a weekend of camping with that same family. However, she had no intention of going camping alone.

Paris was so much better! She knew how to navigate the city, and she knew how to speak French well enough even though, she knew that over time, there would be some changes in how it was spoken. However, she was confident that she could get along.

This time, she had booked her room in advance, not wanting to repeat the same mistake she had made on her first trip. She also knew that this would be her last trip to Paris. Like the first time, she was alone. She didn't have to see everything, just her favorite things.

CHAPTER THREE

WHEN MELISSA GOT off of the plane, she had a small panic attack! The airport was much busier than she had remembered. Taking several deep breaths, she proceeded to baggage claim, retrieved her luggage and exited the airport to find a taxi. She greeted the driver and handed him the address of the hotel in which she would be staying. Using his mirror, the driver made eye-contact with her and smiled.

"Vous-etes d'ou?" (Where are you from?) He asked.

"D'Etats-Unis, Californie." (The United States, California). She answered.

"Etiez-vous, jamais en France avant?" (Have you ever been to France before?) He continued.

"Mais oui. J'adore La France et espe'cialement, Paris!" (Of course, I love France and especially, Paris.) She responded, smiling back into the mirror. "Meme, j'ai ete ici cinq fois." (I have been here 5 times.) She continued. The driver smiled broadly. The conversation continued. He asked if she was meeting or staying with someone. She told him the she had come alone, and would probably be studying at the university, and wouldn't have much time for socializing. He commented that that was a pity because Paris was a "place for lovers."

When they arrived at her hotel, she paid the driver and offered him a tip. He declined saying that she wasn't really a tourist, and he wouldn't take the tip from her. She thanked him as he helped carry her bags into the hotel lobby. Marissa registered and went to her room. The stress of the trip had tired her out, so she laid down on the bed and was asleep as soon as her head hit her pillow. Though it was early afternoon, she slept until morning.

When the sun hit her face, she awakened, and for a split second she panicked again when looking at the unfamiliar surroundings. Then she smiled. She was in Paris! She had really come again!

She showered, dressed and then went down to the lobby to have breakfast. The room was full of chatty tourists. She was glad to see that two tables were empty. One was in the corner, so after getting her coffee, croissant and eggs, she went and sat down at that one, with her back to the wall. She had really wanted to put her back to the crowd, but she knew that that would bring her even more attention than she had already gotten, having been the only African American seated at the tables. The tourists were old, Caucasian and rich-looking. The servants were from The Caribbean: Quadalupe, St. Croix or Martinique. They looked at her curiously, but knew that she was a tourist from America, the word had spread. She greeted them in French and responded with "merci" whenever they did something for her. By being friendly and appreciative when they served her eggs and poured her café', she knew that for the rest of her visit, she would receive special treatment. Too often, she had found that American tourists were rich, rude, and arrogant, and considered these beautiful people to be inferior to themselves. She thought of her mother's favorite Bible saying. She had always told Melissa her version of The Golden Rule. Instead of "do unto others as you would have them do unto you." Her mother would say: "treat people like you want to be treated."

Several of the tourists spoke, so she responded and smiled. She knew that eventually, someone who "had a black friend" would try to befriend her, but today, they just seemed to be watching her, watching to see if anyone would sit with her. So, she ate alone.

After breakfast, she decided that she didn't need to waste time taking a French class. She knew that she was proficient enough, and realized that unless she lived in Paris she would never speak like a native. She also decided that she would do what she had planned to do which was visit a different tourist site every day for the 28 days that she had left, and then she would probably never see Paris again.

Today, she would relax, study her maps, plan her days, and in the afternoon, walk the streets near her hotel. She knew that visiting La Maison de Rodin (Rodin's House) would be the first attraction that she would visit. She loved his sculpture called "The Kiss". The first time she had seen it, it had embarrassed her. She had been so young and inexperienced. She had felt hypnotized by it. She had never seen a naked man before. So, this time, she would be allowed to study the body for as long as she liked. She had only visited the house once. Though the house held no fascination for her, she did want to see if, or how much it and the gardens had changed.

On her third day, she decided to ride the Metro, but after ascending the stairs to the street, she realized that she was lost! Many of the streets were circular, so the idea of making 4 turns to get back to where you started didn't work. In her frustration, she saw a Gendarme (French Policeman). She approached him from the back, and when he turned around she had to catch her breath! He was beautiful! He was tall, with bright white teeth, and a coffee brown complexion. His hair was ebony and wavy. When she composed herself, she asked for directions back to the hotel. He obviously knew how attractive he was, because he flirted with her, and asked her to meet him for coffee the next day. She had been flattered; however, once back at the hotel the red flags went up! She had thought about how dangerous it would be to start a relationship with someone knowing that she would be returning home. So, she had done what she had usually done in any difficult situation. She had run!

Why had she gone alone again? Suddenly, she was having second thoughts. She had never been able to talk any of her friends into going, and tours didn't allow you to explore on your own. She knew the sites would only look more worn and dingy, but speaking French with the "natives", was so enjoyable to her, and she loved Paris! She loved the history of it, the architecture, the mood, the cafe's, riding the Metro and walking the curved streets; the smell of the bakeries and the food. She also knew that if she had gone with someone else, then she probably would have spent more time speaking English than French, and she loved speaking French!

Safely in her room, she fell across the bed just to take a short nap before going to dinner. While sleeping, she dreamt of the sights that she would see again: Versailles, Invalides, Notre Dame, Le Musee' D'Armee', etc. She always smiled thinking that even if you were angry and tried to curse at someone, in French, whatever you said still sounded wonderful!

After sleeping longer than she had expected, she got up to go to the bathroom. Then, she returned to her bed, and fell into a deeper sleep. This time she dreamed of Bill. He never aged. He was always smiling and reaching out to her. He never spoke, but she knew he loved her by the way he looked at her. When she awakened this time, her cheeks were damp. She had been crying! She wondered why Bill had ever shown up in her life. Why, if they were only to know each other for a semester? What had been the point? That would be one of the questions she would ask God when she finally met him face to face!

CHAPTER FOUR

ON HER THIRD day, before venturing out; she spent some time reviewing her map of Paris and plans for the day. As she was exiting the hotel she collided with a man who was crossing her path just outside the entrance. The force of the collision caused her to stumble, drop her purse and nearly fall. Luckily, the man was able to grab her arm, and before she could pick up her purse, he grabbed it too.

"Oh, pardon!" He said still holding her arm to steady her. He handed her purse to her.

"Ça ne fait rien." ("It's nothing.) She responded.

"Bonne journée." ("Good Day".) He said while bowing slightly. He looked at her as if to see if she were hurt, then he smiled, stepped past her, and continued walking in the direction in which he had been going.

Melissa stood in the doorway briefly straightening her clothes, and trying to regain her composure. She looked down the street for the man. She found him easily because he had stopped and turned to look back at her. She saw him smile and then turn back to continue on his way. After she'd lost sight of him, she walked to the Metro, descended the stairs and bought her ticket. She was feeling much more comfortable, having had the good sense to study the map of the Metro stops while waiting for the train.

She found La Maison de Rodin and her favorite sculpture," The Kiss". Even though things were worn, as she had expected, she still enjoyed walking through the house and gardens. She sat in the garden for quite a while breathing in the smells of the flowers and soaking up the peace and beauty of it. When she felt evening was coming, she headed back to her hotel.

Back in her room, she found herself thinking about the man who had crashed into her that morning. He had interrupted her thoughts most of the day. He had been a very attractive Black man. Actually, he had been gorgeous! He had been tall, slender, and well-dressed. His complexion had been the color of Hershey's chocolate and he'd had close-cut salt and pepper gray hair. His eyes were what had struck her the most, because they had been a piercing black. He had had long eyelashes and beautiful naturally arched brows. But it had been the way that he had looked at her and held her gaze that she found herself thinking about him. She couldn't describe the look, but she knew that he seemed reluctant to release her. Then having caught himself, he bowed, apologized and turned to continue on his way. The fact that he had bowed to her made her smile. She thought that he must be "quite the gentleman."

She had wanted to call after him, but she'd had no idea what she would have said to him. She had been attracted to him immediately; because he had seemed shy, and because he had avoided making eye contact with her, yet he had searched her face as if he hadn't believed that she wasn't hurt.

She had stood where he had left her watching him get farther and farther away. She hadn't been able to move! Then when he had suddenly turned to face her, and she saw him smile, her heart had nearly stopped! She had felt paralyzed! She had opened her mouth, but no sound had come. Then just as suddenly, he had turned back around, and continued walking away from her, disappearing into the crowd.

"Wow!" She thought to herself, concern, and admiration in just one glance! When his look had intensified, she had suddenly thought of Bill. She desperately hoped that she would see the man again. Or were "the gods" teasing her once more?

Melissa settled into her routine, and did her best to put the man out of her thoughts. She doubted that she would ever see him again. So, mornings, she would have her breakfast which usually consisted of scrambled eggs, a croissant and a cup of café au lait. It was so delicious, that she usually sat for at least an hour eating and reviewing her plan for the day. Afterwards, she would set off for an attraction, have lunch, then walk around the streets until she felt evening approaching. Each evening, she would select a restaurant near her hotel in which she would have a light dinner. Then she would return to her room, shower, put on her pajamas and lay across her bed where she would watch something on TV, until fell asleep.

By her fifth day, she felt courageous enough to deviate from her usual schedule: hotel to tourist site, to her "walk-about," to her hotel. On this day; she decided to go "window shopping." She had always enjoyed shopping at the two most famous department stores: Au Printemps and La Galleria de Lafayette. They could be compared to Macy's and Nordstrom's. They were in the same area, so that you could walk from one store to the other. However, she spent so much time in Au Printemps, that she decided to come back another day to visit the other store.

While walking to The Metro, she had the uneasy feeling that she was being followed. She didn't dare turn around to look, but she did decide to ignore the feeling and walk a little faster. She was convinced that the reason that she felt like she was being followed was because she did not look "Parisian". Even though she spoke French almost fluently, she knew that her clothes were not stylish enough, so that she wasn't quite "fitting in".

Perhaps she wasn't being followed, just noticed. She was

a curiosity. She descended the Metro staircase, purchased her ticket, then walked to where the trains were to be boarded. As she boarded the train, she put the feeling out of her mind. Thinking about how enjoyable her day had been, put the feeling to rest, and calmed her nerves; however, when she ascended from The Metro to return to her hotel, the feeling resurfaced. She picked up her pace, and not wanting to draw even more attention to herself, she decided not to run; although, that was exactly what she wanted to do.

Once she entered the lobby of her hotel, she felt a sense of relief. The people who worked the front desk seemed to know everyone, and she smiled and spoke to them knowing that no one would be allowed past them if they were not booked at the hotel.

CHAPTER FIVE

PHILLIP WAS SMITTEN, stunned, and interested the moment he looked into the women's large brown eyes. He couldn't stop thinking about her! He had not been paying attention. He had been rushing to a business appointment when he had crashed into her just outside her hotel.

She had attracted him immediately. Her look had been apologetic, as if she had crashed into him. She seemed shy, avoiding making eye contact with him. Most women would have cursed him, or been angry at him, or flirted with him.

But, in looking into her eyes, he had, perhaps, held her a little too long. Then, when he had handed her purse to her, their hands had touched. It was then that the woman had looked at him, and it was then, too, that he had felt a shock! It was like an electric current had traveled through her to him. He was done for!

"Oh, I'm so sorry! Pardonnez-moi!" She had stammered, as he grabbed her to keep her from falling to the pavement. He smiled to himself remembering that it had been all his fault, and yet she had apologized to him.

Her eyes had flashed fear, forgiveness, and admiration in just one glance. "I should have been more careful, stepping out of the hotel into morning traffic." She said in French. She half-smiled at him while placing her purse strap over her shoulder. Then she had stepped back from him, but held his gaze. Reluctantly, he bowed, then continued on his way.

Philip knew how he looked. He knew that he was considered handsome by most women, but just once he wished a woman could see past his looks, his designer clothes and see him, see his heart. He dressed for his job, and he had been promoted to the top because he had worked harder than anyone. Often, he found his looks to be a hindrance instead of a help.

Now, he was ready to share his life with someone, but not just anyone! He wanted a woman he could pursue and win, someone trying to live as God had asked, not someone who sprung on him the minute he glanced in her direction!

The woman this morning had given him hope! He felt like a schoolboy with his first crush! He had to find her! He had to see her again! She acknowledged his looks with the appreciation in her eyes, but that's where she had stopped. She had not flirted with him, or even tried to hold on to him with frivolous conversation. She had simply apologized, unnecessarily, because he had run into her.

He needed to see her again! He didn't know her name, but he assumed that she was staying at the hotel where he had crashed into her. So, he formulated a plan. He wasn't very good at pursuing a woman. He had never had to do so, but this time he realized that he couldn't let her get away! He smiled to himself, thinking that he had prayed so long for a companion that God had finally said "here" and thrown her at him!

Though it was out of his way, he started walking past her hotel in the morning at around the same time he had first seen her, looking for her. He started stopping for coffee in the nearby cafe in the evenings. Three days had passed, and he was becoming anxious! On Philip's fourth morning, as he sat in the café drinking coffee, she emerged from the hotel! He was so excited that he jumped up and almost knocked the table over. He quickly paid for his meal, and started to follow her, but he made sure he was a comfortable distance behind. She walked to the Metro, descended the stairs and bought her ticket. He did the same.

Melissa found that "The man" was also consuming her thoughts. She wondered if she would ever see him again; she tried to put him out of her mind, but she couldn't. She reminded herself that, she was only going to be in Paris for a short time, and getting to know someone would be problematic. But, no matter what she told herself, she still couldn't stop thinking about him.

She took the Metro to Les Invalides (The Army Museum), but she hardly paid attention to the exhibits. She just walked around in a slight daze, and when it was time for lunch, she ate in the museum café, then she went to the gift shop to purchase some souvenirs, and when it was early evening, she took the Metro back to the hotel.

The day after the encounter with the gentleman, she decided to spend at La Galleria.

She had been browsing for a while, when all of a sudden, she heard someone screaming "does anyone speak English?" She looked up to see a large Caucasian man in a Hawaiian Shirt, sandals and socks, with two cameras hanging around his neck. His face was red with frustration, and he was getting angrier by the minute. He was yelling at the woman who was behind the counter, who kept denying that she spoke any English.

When the man saw Melissa, he ran over to her to ask the same question, but by now he was attracting a great deal of attention, and she didn't want to draw attention to herself, so she smiled and responded in French that she didn't speak English. (She hoped that God would forgive her for her "little white lie".) Not finding anyone to translate for him, he stormed off saying some not so nice things about The French.

Melissa knew that the saleswoman spoke some English, because she had been speaking to her in English and French, and she had been responding in both English and French just before the man had entered the store. When the man was gone, the sales clerk smiled and said. "I would never let him know that I spoke English because he was so rude! He could have at least made an effort to speak French. He could have Googled what he wanted to say." She explained to Melissa.

Melissa smiled and responded that she understood. She remembered that French people could be like that. They were very proud of their language, and they didn't like tourists who hadn't bothered to learn any French at all!

After leaving the store, she decided to take a stroll. She had paused to look at a shoe display when she noticed a man had stopped and was looking at the same display. However, the display was clearly to catch the attention of women, so she was curious as to why this man had stopped to look as well. Melissa looked at the man's reflection in the window. He was a tall, slender Black man. His complexion was the color of Hershey's Chocolate. His hair was close cut and salt and pepper gray. He was gorgeous! He reminded her of the man who had collided with her in her hotel doorway, but she thought to herself that it couldn't possibly be him since it would have been an uncanny coincidence. She could tell that he was looking at her by looking at their reflection. She froze! Should she speak? Should she move? After a few seconds, she turned in his direction and smiled. He smiled back.

"It is you!" She said.

"So, you speak English?" He asked.

"Yes, I am American." Melissa explained.

"I used to be." He responded with a half-smile.

"Why do you say that you 'used to be'?" Melissa asked, curiously.

"I have lived here in Paris for the last 35 years." He explained. "I only go back to the U.S. once in a while to visit the last little bit of family that I have left. I came over here with my job and I fell in love with Paris. This is my home now. I don't think that I will ever live in the U.S. again." He said it with such finality, that Melissa didn't know what to say.

"I guess that I can understand that, if I had a job here and little or no family left. But, I have 4 grandchildren that I adore, and I couldn't live more than a couple of months without seeing them." She commented.

"How old are they?" He asked.

"There are three girls 7, 9 and 11, and a little boy of 4." She continued. "I never thought that I would be a grandmother. I was near 30 when my youngest son was born, and my oldest son never married. They are very precious to me." She ended.

"You must have pictures?" He asked. Melissa pulled her one family photo out of her wallet, and showed it to him. "I can see why you love them. They are precious." He said.

Melissa felt that she didn't want to get to know this man who seemed to have turned his back on the United States. Although she, too, loved Paris, she did not want to forsake her homeland. She could admit that America had its problems, but it was still home.

"Well, it was very nice talking to you, but I must be going." She was trying to make her escape. She made a move to leave when he spoke again.

"Although I don't plan on going back, I would love to talk to you more about what is happening in the US. You can, as they say, 'bring me up to speed.'" He said with a half-smile on his face.

"Well, I am only going to be here for a month, actually, twenty-five days now, and I have planned out each day, so I don't think that I can spare any time." She explained, hoping he would understand.

"What if I go along with you, then we can talk and I can be your guide?" He offered.

"I don't even know you. I don't know your name. You could

be an ax-murderer who is running from the law." She knew she sounded a little ridiculous, but she was trying to make her point.

"Oh pardonne!" He said as he smiled and reached in his coat pocket to withdraw a business card. "My name is Philip Nance. Here is the company from which I retired. You can call and they will give you my references. I still check in with them from time to time to do some part-time work. If you want to take me up on my offer, call me. I would love to be your companion for the time that you will be here. It would give me great pleasure." Then he smiled! It was her undoing!

"Well, it has been a pleasure meeting you, Philip. My name is Melissa Matthews." She reached out her hand to shake his. He held it for what she felt was longer than usual, and he held her glance just long enough to make her uncomfortable.

"I hope to hear from you very soon." He said as he continued to hold her gaze. Then, he turned and walked away.

CHAPTER SIX

MELISSA TOOK A day to think about Philip's offer. She didn't really want to get to know anyone, knowing that she would be leaving soon. However, she couldn't stop thinking about him. He was handsome, tall, soft-spoken, educated, and seemingly well off. He had to be, to be living in Paris itself. Yet, she was fearful that he must have some flaw, especially if her were interested in her. That is what her head was telling her; but, her heart was telling her something different.

The next morning, she decided to give him a call. When she did, she got his answering machine, so she left a message for him. When she was about to leave her room for breakfast, her phone rang.

"Salut, Melissa." It was Philip.

"Salut. I have decided to take you up on your offer." She informed him.

"Have you had breakfast?" He asked.

"No, I was just about to go downstairs to the dining room." She responded.

"It would give me great pleasure if you would join me for breakfast. I have a car, I will pick you up in about 15 minutes." He said.

"I will wait for you in the lobby." She replied. As soon as she hung up, she began to feel like she had made a big mistake! This man was a stranger! What had she been thinking! To calm herself, she prayed a small prayer. Then she grabbed her purse and phone and went downstairs to the lobby to wait for him.

In exactly 15 minutes a small car pulled up in front of the hotel. Melissa walked quickly to the car. The hotel doorman opened the passenger door. Before getting in, she bent down to make sure that it was Philip. The car was smaller than Melissa had expected. It was like a toy! She was so close to Philip that their thighs would have been touching had it not been for the stick shift between them. When he shifted the car into neutral, his hand accidently brushed against her thigh, and in true French fashion he immediately and apologetically said, "oh, pardonne!"

"No problem." Melissa responded in French. It could not be helped. What she didn't tell Philip was that she was touched by how embarrassed he seemed to be. However, because she didn't make a big deal out of it, he relaxed a bit, though he suddenly seemed nervous.

"Which site would you like to see today?" He asked. "If you haven't eaten; we can have breakfast nearby." He suggested.

Although she had wanted to go to see The House of Rodin again, she didn't think it would be a good idea until they got to know each other. She didn't want to be embarrassed in front of him, and she certainly, didn't want to put any ideas into his head. Although he seemed nice, she didn't know him well enough yet.

"How about Notre Dame?" She responded. She decided that that would be a good way to let Philip know that she was a Christian, and she could begin to find out about him and his faith. Why his salvation was important to her, she didn't quite know, but she felt that she might be "safer" socializing with him if he were.

"Notre Dame it is!" He said, turning to smile at her.

"That sounds wonderful!" She said, as he pulled away from the curb.

Philip was a good driver. Some streets were so narrow; she marveled at his skills. Others were large "boulevards". It was on the large streets that she could relax. She had questions that she wanted to ask, but he seemed to need the quiet in order to concentrate, so she just looked out the window. Soon she saw The Seine and the Cathedral of Notre Dame.

"Wow!" She commented. "I never get tired of seeing these sites."

"Admittedly, I never do either." Philip said. "I hope you wore comfortable shoes. The last time I was here, the line had a two hour wait."

"Oh, I did." Said Melissa. "Remember, I have been here before." She said, turning her head in order to smile at him. Philip glanced at her shoes and smiled, but when he scanned her legs, she felt a shiver run through her entire body!

Philip was quite the gentleman though. He held her elbow whenever they had to cross a street, or pass a crowded area. It made her feel like they were almost a couple. Remembering the time that she had come with her younger son made her smile. Philip noticed it.

"Have I said something funny?" He asked. He was smiling himself, because he knew that he hadn't said anything at all.

"No, I was remembering when I brought my youngest son here. He was about thirteen at the time. I had a wonderful time with him. He brought an old camera because he said that he had to take pictures for his photography class. However, the only pictures that he took were of pretty young women. He didn't photograph not one site." Smiling, she continued. "When we got off the Metro to walk to Notre Dame, I guess we were too close to it, because I just couldn't find the entrance. We had a map, so I stopped a gentleman and asked him where it was on the map, and which way we should walk. He looked at the map and waved his hand to say that we should turn around and go the other way. We walked and walked and still couldn't seem to find it. Then I noticed that we were getting farther and farther away. All of a sudden I just burst out laughing because I realized that I had been holding the map up-side-down, and so we were walking in the opposite direction."

"That is funny!" He said. "When I first came here, I, too, got lost many times; however, I was too stubborn to ask for directions. I wore out lots of pairs of shoes until I got Paris down."

"I think the fact that many of the streets are circular is the problem." She added.

"Yes, and refusing to use maps correctly doesn't help." Now Phillip was chuckling.

Melissa noticed that he had a wonderful laugh. He didn't snort of make funny noises. He just seemed to laugh with his entire body, without much sound. "I soon learned to study and plan the route I was going to take the night before." He explained.

"Good idea." She agreed, not telling him that that had been her plan before they met. After parking, Philip got out of the car and came around to her side to help her get out.

"Let's grab a croissant and café' before we go in." Philip suggested.

"That would be great! I am kind of hungry." She told him.

Suddenly, Philip took her hand to lead her across the street. She was touched by the gesture. His hand was warm and strong. They sat outside and chatted about what they liked most about Notre Dame. After an hour, they returned to the cathedral to take the tour. As they walked through, Philip constantly held her hand, or placed his hand on the small of her back to guide her through the crowds. She was keenly aware of each time he touched her, but she was sure he had no idea of how his touch was affecting her.

Finally, the tour was over! As they walked back to his car, he took her hand again.

"Where are we going tomorrow?' He asked.

"How about The Louvre?" She asked.

"Sounds good to me." He responded, then he continued. "I just can't understand what the big deal is with The Mona Lisa. People line up to see her, and between you and me, she is pretty homely." He commented.

"I think so too, but it's tradition to see her, and to have her half-smile at you." She added. Then she continued. "So, we must. However, my favorite painting is of Napoleon Crossing the Alps."

"It's huge!" Philip commented.

"That's part of what I like about it. It's almost like Napoleon is there on that horse. Would you like to hear another story?" She asked.

"I'm beginning to love your stories." Philip said, turning to look at her just long enough to make her heart beat a little faster.

"Well, this is a short one," she said softly. "I came with a cousin by marriage a couple of years ago. We had a wonderful time except she snored horribly, so I didn't get much sleep. She took a lot of pictures and posters, and promised to send me the copy of this one of Napoleon. That was ten years ago, and I am still waiting." She ended.

"Let me buy it for you." Philip offered.

"Oh, no!" Melissa said, then added. "Fool me once."

Again, Philip laughed as he grabbed her hand to cross the street. Melissa couldn't believe that she was feeling some sadness that their day together seemed to be ending.

In no time at all they were back at her hotel. Grabbing the door handle, she turned to Philip and said, "Thank you for a wonderful day!"

"It was my pleasure! I enjoyed it more than you know." He said as he smiled and looked at her a little longer than necessary. When Melissa made a move to open the door, Philip quickly opened his door and got out to run around the car to open the door for her. Then, he grabbed her hand and lifted her up so that she was facing him.

"Shall I pick you up tomorrow at about the same time?" He asked.

"That would be nice!" Melissa answered. For an awkward moment, Philip just stood there looking down at her. Not knowing what he was going to say or do, Melissa spoke.

"Then I will see you tomorrow."

"Yes." He seemed unable to move, so she stepped past him to enter the hotel.

"What am I doing?" Melissa mumbled to herself as she entered the elevator. Philip was handsome, cultured, smart, tall, and had the blackest eyes she had ever seen! When he looked at her, she felt that he could see through her to her heart, and her soul. "I need to stop this before it is too late!" She thought, desperately wanting to turn back to see if he had driven off.

Once in her room, she suddenly felt very tired. She took off her clothes, wrapped herself in her robe and lay on the bed. Before she realized it, she was asleep. Once asleep, she dreamed of Philip. He was smiling, and holding his arms out to her, saying "come to me, my love", but with each step that he made towards her, he seemed to get farther and farther away. She awakened with her heart racing. Then she realized that it was the first time, in a long time, that she had not dreamt of Bill.

The next morning, she showered and dressed and was ready when Philip pulled up in front of her hotel. As she walked towards his car, he got out to open her door.

"Good morning, Melissa." She loved the way he said her name.

"Good morning, Philip." She responded as she got into his car. Once again, she smelled his cologne. She noted how good he smelled, and how good he looked. He always wore a suit that fitted him well. She would have asked him what the name of his cologne was, but she knew that once she left Paris, she would never want to smell it again, because it would bring up the painful memory of having to leave him.

"Are you okay?" Philip asked. He seemed to sense her mood had changed, though she was smiling at him.

"Yes. I was just thinking of something. Sorry! I am fine." She told him.

With that Philip walked to his side of the car and got in, turned on the ignition, turned to smile at her, and then to pull out into the traffic.

Trying to lighten her mood, Melissa commented on his driving ability. "I would be terrified if something happened to you while we were driving somewhere, and I had to take over. I couldn't do it." She told him. She continued. "The streets are so narrow and the cars are on the wrong side of the road." She explained.

"It's not as terrifying as it seems. The streets are narrow, but the cars are built to fit them." He said, turning to smile at her. "As for 'being on the wrong side of the road', well, you adapt quickly especially after you have had a couple of near head-on collisions." Philip said it like he was speaking from experience. But she didn't ask whether or not he was speaking of himself.

Soon they were at The Louvre, so he turned into a parking spot. It seemed that the entire world was there too. They waited in line to purchase tickets, and ascended the escalator to the main floor. All the while, Phillip held her hand, or her arm, in order to guide her through the crowds. It touched her, that he was so protective, when they had really just met.

After about an hour, they decided that they probably wouldn't get to see much that day because of the crowds, so Philip suggested, that they come back another day to finish touring. Walking to a nearby café', they stopped for lunch and talked about other favorite things they would want to see in the Louvre when they returned. Philip paid for their meal, then they walked back to his car.

"I am so grateful that I met you. I have always been rushed, and unable to enjoy myself." She didn't want to tell him that she had often come alone, and that being with him now, had made Paris look different, newer and more interesting. It was as if she was seeing everything for the first time.

"And, I can't tell you how much I am enjoying being your guide, Melissa." Philip said, as he reached for her hand in her lap. Then, he turned to look at her. His look was intense. She felt hypnotized by it. She couldn't move, and could hardly breathe. He released her hand, and pulled the car into the traffic. They rode in silence to her hotel. Philip pulled to the curb, and put the car into neutral. He seemed reluctant to let her out.

"Thanks so much!" She whispered. "I look forward to seeing you tomorrow."

"I don't think I can wait until tomorrow." He said softly. "Would you have dinner with me?" Melissa knew that she was beginning to like him very much, but in her heart, she was afraid that if she fell in love with him, things would get complicated.

"I don't know, Philip. Do you think that is a good idea?" She asked looking at his profile.

"I think it is a very good idea. I am sure you plan to eat this evening, and I am definitely going to do so, it's just that we will be doing it together." When he said it like that, it sounded so simple. She was embarrassed that she had possibly read anything more into his request.

"Then, I will pick you up at 6:00 pm, okay?" He asked.

"That will be fine." She responded.

"Great." He said, bringing her hand to his lips. He kissed it, got out of the car and came around to open the door for her. Once out of the car she turned to face him.

"Thank you for a lovely afternoon!" She said.

"It was my pleasure, and I look forward to dinner with you this evening." He reached for her hand and kissed it again. Marissa felt a tingle run through her body, but she tried not to show that his kiss had affected her. She smiled, turned and walked to the lobby.

CHAPTER SEVEN

MELISSA THOUGHT THAT a nap might do her good; so, she laid across her bed. She immediately fell to sleep. When she awakened, she headed straight for the mirror. "What does he see in me?" She asked her reflection. Her heart was beating, and tears had welled up in her eyes. She was frightened, frightened that she would fall in love with Philip, and her past experiences would repeat themselves. He was too handsome! He was too educated! He was too accomplished to be truly interested in her. He was probably just doing what he had initially said. He was just trying to catch up on news from The U.S.

She flopped down on the bed face down, and cried. When she felt that she had exhausted all of her tears she pushed off of the bed to look at the clock. Her room was dark. It was 5:30 PM. Philip was coming at 6:00 PM! At break-neck speed she showered and dressed. Her hair was never a problem. She wore a short Afro. It was, like Philip's, salt and pepper; her eyes large and brown. She outlined her eyes again, put on some lipstick and sat down on the bed to wait for the phone to ring. Promptly at 6:00 PM, it did so.

"Salut Melissa, I am here." Philip said into the receiver. His voice seemed deeper, more seductive. It made her heart skip a beat to hear it.

"I'll be right down." She said, with a lump in her throat. When she walked into the lobby after getting out of the elevator, she could see Philip. He seemed nervous. She found his nervousness sweet. He stood, smiled and walked toward her. He was wearing a black suit, white shirt and gray tie. Everything he had on looked crisp and clean. He took her hand, kissed it, and smiled.

"You look beautiful!" He said.

"Thank you!" It nearly caught in her throat. She thought that he looked beautiful too. But she didn't say it. She didn't think a man would appreciate being told that, so all she said was, "you don't look so bad yourself!"

Philip laughed, and kissed her hand again.

"Le Jules Verne." He responded, not telling her that it was inside the Eiffel Tower. As they walked to his car, he held her hand. They chatted lightly about the day, but Melissa felt that the weight between them was getting heavy; that neither was willing to talk about what was happening between them.

The restaurant was indescribably beautiful! She couldn't imagine how much dinner would cost, so she tried to find something on the menu that didn't seem too expensive. Philip smiled at her as if he seemed to know what she was thinking.

"Don't worry." He said softly. "I wouldn't have brought you here if I couldn't have afforded it." He smiled.

"How did you know what I was thinking?" She asked.

"I guess I am beginning to know how you think, and it amazes even me." He said. "It's like I have been waiting for you all my life." His look was intense, his tone soft and seductive.

Although the meal was delicious, the way that Philip kept looking at her made swallowing difficult. He held her eyes when she spoke and often glanced at her mouth and throat. She noticed that he controlled his eyes, so that she never caught him looking at her breasts. She had never met a man like him. She knew that her feelings for him were growing past "friendship "but, she couldn't help herself.

Every time he reached for something, she couldn't help looking at his strong hands, his broad chest, his dark eyes... Her breath would catch in her throat. She wanted to run out of the room, she felt that she couldn't breathe, but she didn't want to make a scene, so she smiled and took several long, slow breaths.

"Are you okay?" Philip asked softly while reaching across the table for her hand.

"I...am...just a little ...overwhelmed by the beauty of this restaurant, the view, the dinner." Her voice was now a whisper.

"You're welcome." Philip said, as he smiled broadly.

"After all of the times that I have been to Paris, I never had the nerve to tour the Eiffel Tower. I am not really good with heights. This is something that I will never forget." She continued. Her voice softened to a whisper.

"It sounds like you are saying good-bye." He, too, spoke softly.

"No, not good-bye." She explained. "It's just I don't think anything else we do, or see will top this evening. Thank you."

"Is that a challenge?" Philip asked, his eyes boring into hers, his lips smiling.

"No...I, I, I, only meant that I have seen the other sites, but this, I've never seen, or experienced before."

"Again, you're welcome."

They finished their dinner with little conversation. It seems that each felt that this was a turning point. They both knew that this "casual relationship" that they had planned, was morphing into something more, and they couldn't seem to do anything about it.

After dinner, Philip held her hand as they walked to his car. They rode in silence, each seemingly lost in thought. When he pulled up in front of her hotel, he turned off the engine, then turned to look at Melissa.

"Don't go just yet." He said. "Can we sit here a while and talk?" He asked.

"I'd like that." Melissa's voice was barely a whisper. "I can't thank you enough for such a beautiful evening."

Philip didn't look at her, he just stared directly ahead as if he was fascinated by the evening lights. She could see his jaw pulsing, as if he were trying to hold back his words.

"What is it, Philip?" She asked.

"Are you sure you want to know what I am thinking?" He turned to look at her, his smile sensuous. His eyes intense. He reached for her hand, then continued. "I know that we have only known each other for a little while, but every time we part I feel that I have lost something precious, and I can't wait to see you again."

Melissa turned her head away from him so that he couldn't see the tears that were welling up in her eyes. She blinked repeatedly until she felt that they wouldn't run down her cheeks.

"Oh Philip, that's the nicest thing anyone has ever said to me." She said softly.

Suddenly, Philip smiled. "Let's go somewhere together, away from Paris. Just the two of us." He continued. "Somewhere we can be together without interruptions. Somewhere with no crowds." He explained. "I feel that we are meant to be more than what we are right now; more than "tour guide and tourist."

"But, I thought you were just going to be my tour guide. Why do you want to test our relationship? You have become a dear friend to me."

"Is that all I have become to you, your 'friend'"? This time she saw it; "the look". It made her feel naked! His eyes didn't move from hers, but the burning in them made her feel warm all over. It was the look that Bill had given her, all those years ago! Her cheeks were warm with the intensity of it!

"Oh!" was all that escaped from her.

"Obviously you don't know how attractive I find you." He continued. "I haven't slept well since our first encounter." He continued.

"I was trying not to notice how you look at me." She said softly. "My dreams haven't been all that chaste either." She was embarrassed, but wanted to be honest. Philip threw his head back and laughed.

"Oh, Melissa!" His voice was deep and seductive. His eyes boring into hers. "Scouts honor. You will be safe. I promise, just one weekend. There are so many places we can get to in just a few hours. That is one of the pleasures of being in Europe. Where would you like to go? Germany, Switzerland, Italy, you name it." He asked.

Melissa couldn't protest. The thought of having Philip all to herself without any distractions excited her. "I remember a very nice beach in Nantes." She told him. "I never shared with you that I had come before and lived with two families when I was in college. It is a very long story, and I will tell you about it, but for now suffice it to say that the one family, that called me their "adopted American daughter" moved out of Paris to a place close to Nantes called St. Brevin, L'Oce'an when the father retired. I spent a Spring there with them."

"What happened to them?"

"Oh, they died a long time ago. I have never seen or been around two people who loved each other so much! The last time I visited them, the husband told me that he had cancer and was dying. We were at the airport in Nantes when he told me and said "good-bye" to me. The wife basically lost her mind after he died. Her daughter had to come get her and move her into her home. She lives in Southern France. She wrote me several times, that her mother asked about her dad every day until she died."

"Sounds like quite a love story." Philip commented.

"Yes, it was. They were the reason I could come to France so often. I always lived with them, and all I had to pay for was my airfare. I miss them very much."

"Where else have you been?" Philip asked.

"Well, I met the 2 families the first time. The second time, I spent 8 weeks studying in Lausanne, Switzerland, at the University of Lausanne. It was grueling! We studied 8 hours per day for 8 weeks! I came with an airplane full of college students from all over the US., and by the end of the session, I was the only one still going to class! The best part was that on the weekends, we could hop on a train and go as far as we could get, as long as we were back in time for class on Monday mornings. So, I was able to travel to Germany, Austria, and Italy." She continued. "I had met a girl from Boston, her name was Heather. We hitchhiked from Lausanne to Munich, Germany. It took 22 hours. We rode with a trucker who spoke no English, a German mother and son who spoke neither French nor English, and a rich German gentleman who did speak English, who took us on a tour of Germany. He showed us a Roman Colosseum there. He was the owner of watch company. He was very rich, and very nice. I think his car was either a Mercedes or a Porche. I still can't believe that I did that! After we got to Germany we had to rush back to school, so we took the train. Then to top it all off, the lady in charge of our group ran off with an Italian young man, and left me in charge of the group! She said that I was the only one who could do it because I was the only one who really spoke French well enough to explain the situation. I had to get them all to England where we were to fly home."

Philip listened attentively, smiling at how animated she had become. He seemed unable to tear his eyes away from her mouth as she talked. He was enjoying hearing about her past. He felt he was getting to know her more deeply.

Melissa abruptly stopped to apologize for dominating the conversation for so long. She felt that perhaps she had talked too much.

"You have had a pretty interesting life." He said. "I can't wait until we are alone. I want to hear more. I wish I had been there with you. I haven't seen much of anything, because I worked quite long hours, and I often had to work Saturdays." He continued. Even though I've lived here a long time, I only speak English and French, and I haven't been as brave as you were. I don't like traveling to places where I can't speak the language." He commented.

"It's late, Philip. I'd better go inside. We can talk more on our excursion. Nantes, then?" Melissa asked.

"If that is your choice, yes."

"This weekend, then?"

"Yes, may I kiss you good-night?" Melissa was surprised!

"Yes, that would be nice." Philip put his arm around her shoulders, then drew her closer.

"This won't work!" He said, so he got out of the car and came to open Melissa's door. He took both of her hands and lifted her up, then he slid his arms around her waist and drew her to him. His kiss was gentle, but it stirred her. She felt that she had been kissed before, but never like this! His lips were soft, and he smelled wonderful, and he held her like no one ever had. He held her like she was something precious.

"You can open your eyes now." He said softly, smiling down at her. His eyes were dark, and intense. Not wanting the evening to end, she spoke.

"I don't have any casual clothes to wear. I don't even have any shorts or Bermuda pants, or pants period. I just packed dresses, skirts, and such, because I didn't expect to dress casually. It's Paris after all. So, tomorrow, I need to go shopping instead of touring." She explained.

"Since it's my idea, I insist that you allow me to purchase some things for you."

"Oh no! I couldn't let you to do that!" She was horrified that he would learn what size she was! She was no longer the young slim women she had never been! She had always been, as her parents said, "healthy", thick but not fat.

"I insist. I won't have it any other way. As I said, it is my idea to take this excursion, and I can afford it." He said it with such finality that Melissa didn't argue. Changing the subject, he asked. "Are you nervous?"

"Yes, a little. But I trust you." She said, looking in his eyes.

"I appreciate that. It will be fun." He squeezed her hand, then leaned over to kiss her cheek. "We will shop tomorrow. What time will you be ready?"

"How about 10:00 am?"

"I'll be here."

"Good night, Philip."

"Good night, Melissa. Sweet dreams." He said softly. Then he turned to go get into his car.

CHAPTER EIGHT

ON HER EIGHTEENTH day, Philip texted to confirm that he would pick her up at 10:00 AM since they had stayed up late the previous evening. She texted him back that she would be ready. Today, they would be shopping for casual clothes for their weekend trip to Nantes and St. Brevin- L'Ocean.

She showered and dressed and went down to the lobby for coffee and a croissant. She sat in a spot where she could see him pull up, and when he did so, she exited the hotel and walked swiftly to his car so that he wouldn't have to get out.

"Salut." He said. As she got in. She did her best to do it in a "lady-like" manner. She noticed that Philip glanced at her legs, but immediately turned away. He seemed to be lost in thought as they drove to the department store, so she just looked out of the window. Though he was quiet, it wasn't awkward. She knew that he was thinking about the trip and what they would need. After a few minutes of silence, she spoke.

"Would you like to hear about the other family I stayed with?" She asked.

"Most definitely." He responded taking the opportunity to look at her. He smiled, then turned back to his driving.

"They weren't so much fun! The father was basically a tyrant! Whenever we were discussing something at dinner-time, if someone disagreed with him, he would halt the discussion by pounding on the table and yelling; "ca, suffit la'"! (That's enough!) Then the family, myself included, would tip-toe through the rest of the evening. I was on pens and needles most of the time. There were four children in the family, 2 girls and 2 boys. The oldest was a girl, Anny. She got pregnant and was basically thrown out. I found that out when I went back years later to visit, she was living in Paris, in an apartment.

The oldest boy, Jean-Rene' was given the job of helping me learn French. He took his job seriously, so I didn't hear English until I came home!" She laughed while remembering, then continued; "When I got home I couldn't stop speaking French!" My parents would smile and just look at each other. It took me about 2 weeks or so to re-adjust. Jean-Rene' became a design engineer. He is quite rich now and lives somewhere in Versailles."

"Have you looked him up since you are here?" Philip asked.

"No. I did see him years later. It was on my third trip. That was when I brought my son with his camera. Jean-Rene' took us to lunch at a yacht club. People were falling all over him, and he was quite the aristocrat. The lunch was great, and it was good to see him, but there wasn't much to talk about." She continued. "His wife really wanted to meet me, but I didn't have a car, and I didn't know what I would say to her, so we parted at the Metro, and I lost contact with him after that." She continued. "Sometimes, I can't believe the life that I have had! God has truly blessed me! All because my college French professor encouraged me to go to France." Speaking about God had slipped out! They had not really spoken about faith, God, etc.

Philip smiled. "Yes. God has been good to me as well." He turned to look at her and reached over to squeeze her hand. Melissa was so relieved to hear him say what he had said.

Now, she realized that Philip was a godly man as well as a good man. That is why he was so reluctant to kiss her. Joy welled up within her. *"Handsome, wealthy, tall, kind, and saved!!"* It was too much! She broke into an inner smile, and said a small prayer. *"Dear God, help us, if it is your plan that we be together."*

They drove the rest of the way in silence. At the store, Philip took control, and had her try on whatever he thought would be comfortable and appropriate for the trip. She tried on the clothes he gave her in the dressing room, and came out to model each outfit for him. Having him look her up and down, as well as having her turn slowly, made her feel exposed.

As they walked to his car, with bags in hand, he said very softly; "you are a very beautiful woman, Melissa." No one had ever said anything like that to her, not even either of her ex-husbands!

Again, she was speechless. "And you are a very handsome man." She responded. "I have never known anyone like you. I am so glad we met." Thinking that she had said enough, she just reached for his arm.

He loaded the trunk with the packages, and then helped her into the car. She knew that she was going to miss the way he treated her. She had never, ever been treated with such care. She wondered if it was a mistake to go with him. She wondered if it was a mistake to continue seeing him. She knew she was falling in love with him. She felt like an insect caught in a spider's web. She wanted to flee, but she was stuck.

"Un centime pour vos pensées." (A penny for your thoughts.) He said softly.

She smiled, but didn't share them. When he pulled up to her hotel, he asked.

"Would you like to go out for dinner?"

"No, I think I will pack and write some letters." She responded.

"May I see you tomorrow?" He asked.

"Of course." She didn't want to tell him that she didn't need a road trip to clarify her feelings. She knew she loved him already. However, she would never say so. She also remembered that he had told her that he would never live in the U.S. again, but she hoped that after their time in Nantes, he would change his mind.

"We will do something short tomorrow. I don't want to tire you out before our trip." Philp said. Then he asked. "How about lunch on Les Champs-Elysees?"

"That sounds great!" What time should I be ready?"

"I'll pick you up at Noon."

"I'll be ready." She said reaching for the door handle.

"No! No! Allow me!" Philip was already out of his car. He didn't tell her how much he enjoyed watching her swing her legs around in order to exit the vehicle, or how much he also enjoyed holding her hand to help her stand, and catching a whiff of her fragrance when she did.

When she was standing facing him, he seemed unable to move. He was very close. Closer than he had ever been. She felt his breath on her face. She didn't have the courage to look into his dark eyes. In trying to avoid his eyes, her gaze landed on his mouth, and that was a mistake! She felt her knees give way, and Philip quickly reach around her waist to steady her. He pulled her closer.

"Are you okay?" He asked with concern in his voice.

"I'm okay, just a little tired." She said softly. She wanted to look away, but she was hypnotized.

"Let me help you to the lobby." He said, still holding her around her waist, he pulled her tighter to him to support her weight.

"I am really fine." She couldn't tell him, that he was the cause of her unsteadiness.

"Will you be okay for our trip? Perhaps you are exhausted, and should rest." His concern touched her.

"Philip, I would rather die than miss this trip! I am so looking forward to it! Perhaps I will pass on lunch. We have been going out every day." She reminded him. She couldn't tell him that her exhaustion had nothing to do with their daily excursions, but a great deal to do with her trying to keep things casual. Her emotions were the problem.

"Will you call me tomorrow?" She asked trying to avoid looking at him.

"I will come by to check on you. We can sit in a nearby café, if that is okay."

"I'd like that." She said. The thought of not seeing him was torturous.

"A' demain." He said while bending down to kiss her cheek.

"Oui, a' demain." She responded, sensing warmth where he had kissed her.

CHAPTER NINE

THE NEXT MORNING Melissa stayed in bed, and slept late. Her exhaustion was emotional. On the one hand, she couldn't wait to see Philip, but on the other hand, she felt like packing and running for her life!

She called the front desk and had her breakfast brought to her room after explaining to the concierge that she was not feeling well. By early evening, she had not yet heard from Philip. She was beginning to feel anxious. He had said that he would stop by to check on her. It wasn't like him to not keep his word, or to not call her. Convincing herself that he had probably been called in to work at his old job, she dressed and went downstairs to dine in the café next door.

It had never occurred to her to call him. His number was on her cell phone, but she sensed that something must be wrong, and she didn't want to interrupt him. All the times they had been together, he had always called and been prompt. Even though she was fearful that something had happened, she knew he would call as soon as he could.

After eating, she returned to her room, took a shower, then laid down on the bed to watch TV. She kept checking her cell to see if Philip had texted her, even though she knew it would "ping" if he had. The worry of the day made her sleepy, and she soon fell asleep. Once more she dreamt of Philip. He was running towards her again, and like her previous dream, with each step he seemed to get farther and farther away; except this time, he was calling her name. Then, she was in a forest where she saw him, but got lost and couldn't get to him. When she awakened it was dark, and her heart was pounding. She prayed that he would call.

At 10:00 PM, her phone rang. It was him.

"Melissa, I am so sorry!" He sounded tired and anxious. "It's late, and I didn't want to disturb you, but I need you!" His voice was strained, and he sounded exhausted.

"It's okay, Philip, what has happened?" She asked timidly, almost afraid to hear the reason he was about to give for his absence.

"My neighbor and boss has had a stroke! He has been like a father to me since I relocated here, and I had to get him to the hospital. I am so sorry I didn't call! It has been "touch and go" all day! I didn't want to disturb him by making a call in his room, and I didn't want to not be near if he asked for me. He is in the ICU Ward. It doesn't look good. I need to contact his family. They don't live in Paris, but I am afraid to leave him. The doctor said that he may die! The stroke was severe!" Philip's voice had changed. It was thick with emotion and almost inaudible.

"Oh Philip, what can I do? I am so glad to hear from you. I was so worried! I have been imagining all kinds of things that could have happened to you! Her voice was trembling, and she was holding back her tears."

"I would appreciate it if you would just come and sit with me." He said softly.

"I'll be there within the hour. At what hospital are you?"

"It's the Hospital Paris Saint-Joseph at 185 Rue Raymond Losserand." He continued.

"You don't know how good it makes me feel to hear that you were worried about me." He was deeply touched by her concern for him. His voice was soft. Even though they were on the phone, his voice felt like a caress on her cheek. He continued, "unfortunately, we will have to postpone our trip. I hope you aren't too disappointed."

"It's okay." She reassured him. Then she added. "I'm on my way."

"Thank you, Melissa." He said, speaking softly. "I will call his family when you get here."

Melissa dressed quickly and said a short prayer for this man who Philip obviously cared for so much. Her prayer was short: "Father, I do not know this man, but I know Philip. If he cares for this man, then I am sure he is a good man. I love Philip, and I ask for your healing for Philip's sake; in the name of Jesus Christ."

She had not consciously acknowledged to herself that she loved Philip, but now she did. "I love Philip." That's what she had said in her prayer. The realization set her heart to beating. After dressing quickly, she phoned the hotel desk to ask them to call her a taxi. She was waiting in the lobby when it arrived.

"Hospital Paris–Saint Joseph, 185 Rue Raymond-Losserand, s'il vous plait." She told the driver. It was an easy drive, since it was night. She paid the taxi driver, and entered the hospital. Philip had evidently told the attendants that she was coming, because they were waiting in the lobby to take her to the room.

Melissa waited outside until the attendant went in and spoke to Philip. She could see him sitting by the bed with his head in his hands. When the nurse told him that she was there, he stood quickly and walked to where she was standing just outside the door. He grabbed her immediately and pulled her to him.

"I'm so sorry, Philip." She said, holding him around his waist, she whispered into his chest.

"Thank you for coming. I am so glad that you are here." His voice was ragged with emotion. He buried his face in her neck, then let out a sigh. That single breath made her tingle all over. She hugged him harder.

When he released her, he took her hand, and led her into the room and placed the extra chair next to the one in which he had been sitting. They both sat down, but remained silent.

Melissa had never seen Philip look so tired. His eyes were pink and his clothes were slightly wrinkled. Her heart went out to him. She took his hand in hers and squeezed it. When she did so, he turned to her and smiled wearily.

"It's okay if you don't want to talk. I just want to be here with you." She told him.

Philip reached over and put his arm around her. He looked like he hadn't slept in several days even though it had only been since early that morning that his friend had taken ill.

"Rest if you can. I will let you know if he wakes up." She continued.

"I'll try." Philip said. Then he leaned back to rest his head on the back of the chair and, stretched out his legs which he crossed at his ankles. He seemed to fall immediately asleep.

It was a rare opportunity Philip had given her, to be able to watch him sleep. She scanned him from his foot to his head, and there was nothing she saw that didn't please her. His legs were long and slender, yet muscular; his chest broad, his hands gentle, his face, strong. "*Wow!*" was all that she could think. The thought that he was interested in her, made her sad.

"He must be terribly lonely to think that I am 'beautiful'". She thought to herself. She also felt that she was "out of his league." Sadly, she decided that she would spend every waking moment with him, and when it was time to go, she would go. She released a heavy breath, but resigned herself to her decision.

After about an hour, Philip opened his eyes. When he saw her, he smiled and reached for her hand. "Thanks, again, for coming." He whispered. Then he stood, straightened his clothes and walked over to the bed to see if his friend looked any better. "Has the nurse checked on him?" He asked her quietly.

"Yes, she came in, right after you fell asleep. But, she didn't say anything."

"If you don't mind, I will go call his family. Come and get me if there is any change."

With that, he stepped into the hallway. In about 30 minutes he returned. "They are planning to come tomorrow." He told her. "Let's go get some coffee and something to eat? I have been here since early this morning, and I am starved. The nurse has my cell number, so she can call me if there is any change." Melissa stood and gathered her things. "I must look terrible, but thanks for letting me sleep." He leaned and place a kiss on her cheek.

"I am so glad I could help." She said looking up into his weary eyes.

Philip took her elbow and steered her out of the room. There were several cafes near the hospital. They chose the one where they could see some members of the hospital staff eating. When they had found a place to sit, Melissa asked. "What's your friends name?"

"His name is Jean-Rene'. He owns his own engineering design company, and I moved here to work for him. He was recruiting in The United States and I was one of his interns. He took special interest in me. He taught me his business, and let me live with him and his family until I could find a place to stay. Not only that, he made me part of his family. I owe him everything! He has been like a father to me, when I didn't have one."

Melissa could hear the affection in his voice. She grabbed his hand and squeezed it. After they had eaten, they walked back to the hospital. Philip asked the doctor about Jean-Rene'. The doctor said that he was resting and stable, and that there wasn't much more anyone could do. He ended by saying that Jean-Rene' was "in God's Hands."

"Perhaps it would be best for you to go home and rest." Melissa suggested. "I am sure they will call you if something changes. The doctor is right. There isn't much we can do just sitting here." Then she made a suggestion. "If there is a church around here, perhaps we should take the doctor's suggestion and pray for him. We haven't talked much about our faiths, but I believe God will do what is best for Jean-Rene', and you should take comfort in that."

Philip looked at Melissa and smiled slightly. "I am not sure God would even know me. It has been quite a long time since we spoke. I've always had a deadline to meet or a meeting to attend, so I haven't attended church like I should have, but if you go with me I'd like to pray for Jean-Rene'." With that he took her hand.

In the lobby, Philip asked where the closest church might be, and was directed to a Catholic Church (Our Lady of Rosary) nearby. Since it was so close, they walked. The church was Gothic looking on the outside, but fairly modern inside.

They sat down near the back, and each said a prayer for Jean-Rene'. When they were done, Philip smiled. "I do feel much better, especially with you here with me." Melissa smiled.

"You need to go home and get some rest. The doctor promised to call if there was any change." She reminded him.

"Tomorrow, I will probably need to go to the office and let everyone know of his condition. Even if he pulls through, someone is going to need to step in to help run things until he has recovered." Philip said.

"Is there someone who can?" Melissa asked.

"Yes, there is. Unfortunately, that someone is me. Even though I am semi-retired and only work part-time now, I know his business inside and out. I don't mind except it wouldn't allow me to see you much, and our time is getting short; and we won't be able to take our trip."

Melissa hadn't thought of that! Not seeing Philip, when she

only had two weeks left before she was to return home, would make for a sad couple of weeks; however, she knew that she had to encourage Philip to help his friend.

"We can still see each other every evening. We can have our dinners together. It won't be too bad, and if you don't do this for Jean-Rene' you will never forgive yourself."

She tried to sound bright and cheery, but she was saddened by the prospect of not spending her last few days with Philip like she had been.

"I guess we should have prayed about that as well." Philip tried to smile, but she could see the smile didn't reach his beautiful dark eyes.

They walked back to the hospital. Philip checked with the doctors, and told them that he would be "on-call" at home, and that he would be back the first thing in the morning. He asked them to call him as soon as there was any change, no matter how small. Then, he and Melissa walked to his car.

After starting the engine, Philip turned to Melissa. "Do you have to go to your place? If our time is going to be shortened, I'd like to spend as much time as possible with you. Come home with me. I promise that you will be safe. I just don't particularly want to be alone right now." His eyes were pleading, and she felt so sad for him.

"I trust you, Philip; however, can we stop by my hotel so I can get a change of clothes?"

"Of course, and thank you."

It was nearly midnight when they arrived at his apartment. Melissa was stunned that it was right outside the Seine, near Notre Dame. It finally hit her that Philip must be very well off.

"I know that you said you majored in engineering design, but what kind of work do you do for Jean-Rene'?" She asked as he opened the door to his building.

"Well", he began, "I majored in Business Management, but

for Jean-Rene', I was hired as a management analyst, which means I looked at efficiencies, examined profit margins, and studied the company's structure and personally examined the company's finances so I could totally understand its function and how to make it profitable. I used to do a lot of traveling, and that's why I ended up living here. I was only sent over to work for him a short time, but the job just kept growing, and I got tired of the constant cross-continental travel, so I stayed." He yawned as he finished his sentence.

After unlocking the door to his apartment. He showed her the bathroom, and his bedroom where she would sleep. She immediately went into the bathroom to change into her night clothes. When she came out, she was wearing her gown. But in her haste to pack, she had forgotten her robe. Philip was standing at the window looking out at the night sky. When he heard the bathroom door open, he turned. He scanned her with his dark eyes, and she felt momentarily naked. Then he smiled.

"I will sleep on the couch here by the window." He told her. His voice seemed deeper, softer, and more seductive than she had ever heard.

"You are taller than me, are you sure you don't want your bed?" She was nervous now, realizing that she was in his apartment, and they would be together all night."

"I have slept here many times. Sometimes when I have had an exhaustive day at work, the couch was as far as I could make it."

"Well, good-night, Philip. I will pray again for Jean-Rene'. He is blessed to have you in his life."

"Thank you. I think I am also blessed to have you in my life." He said it as he walked over to her. Her gown was thin. Without her robe, she knew that her body had responded to his look. She felt naked and nervous.

"Do you think I could have a good-night kiss?" His voice was like a caress.

A few minutes ago, his eyes had been pink and he had looked like he was going to collapse. Now, seeing her in her night gown his eyes took on an intensity she had not seen before.

"Scouts honor, just one kiss!" He said it as he pulled her into his arms. His kiss was gentle, sweet, and all that she had hoped it would be. "Melissa, sweet Melissa!" He whispered into her hair. She was afraid to move; to spoil the moment, but she couldn't help but respond to his kiss. She kissed him back, feeling all the love in her heart for this gentle, kind, godly man.

"I'd better stop before I won't be able to." He nuzzled her neck, then pushed her away from him. "Good night, my love." He whispered.

"Goodnight, Philip." She bit her lip so she wouldn't say "I love you!"

"Sleep well." He added.

Melissa walked to his bedroom and closed the door. "How in God's name am I supposed to sleep with him just a few steps away!" She thought. All night she tossed and turned.

In the morning, she was awakened by smells of coffee and warm croissants.

When she walked into the kitchen, she saw that Philip was already dressed. He had his back to her and was doing something at the counter. She was barefoot and he didn't hear her enter the kitchen. She couldn't resist, so she walked up behind him and put her arms around him.

"Good morning." She said resting her head on his back.

"Good morning." He said turning around to hug her. Once again, she felt naked by the way he looked at her.

"Did you sleep well?" He asked.

Melissa was ashamed to admit that she hadn't, and that she had tossed and turned all night, trying to keep from joining him on his couch. It had been a very long time since she had desired a man like she ached for Philip. She couldn't admit that to him, so she just smiled.

"I'll get dressed, then we can have breakfast."

"Take your time." He said softly. "I rather enjoy seeing you walk around in that gown." He continued as he briefly looked her over with a teasing half-smile on his face.

After they had breakfast, Philip dropped her off at her hotel, and said that he would see her at dinner-time, around 6:00 pm., and if her couldn't get away from work, he would let her know when he would be coming. He assured her that no matter what time he got off, he would come to see her.

CHAPTER TEN

MELISSA BUSIED HERSELF until evening. She didn't want to miss Philip's call, and she was afraid that she wouldn't hear her cellphone if she went out into the street. Paris, like most cities, was a busy, noisy place. She wasn't in the mood to go out anyway. She had gotten used to Philip being her guide and companion, and she just didn't want to tour without him. He had spoiled her.

At Noon, he called to tell her that he was on a lunch break, and that he missed her and their time together. He also told her that he had heard from the hospital and Jean-Rene's family. The doctors said his condition had improved, and he might be going home within a week, but that he definitely wouldn't be going back to work for quite some time. He added that Jean-Rene's sister called and said that each family member would stay with Jean-Rene' one week at a time until he could take care of himself, and if he couldn't, one of them would take him in.

"I am so glad that his family has stepped up and made arrangements for his around-the-clock care. That really takes some of my burden away, and it guarantees that we can see each other these last few days. In fact, I think that we can take that trip to Nantes." Philip said.

Melissa was overjoyed to hear it! "Oh Philip, are you sure?" She asked.

"I am more certain than I have ever been about anything." He said. He explained that things were going well at the company, and that he had found someone who, in a few months, might be able to take over the job that he was doing. Although, when that happened, he promised to be around periodically to help out.

"This is my last weekend, and my last week." She reminded him. "I am booked to fly out a week from Monday morning."

There was a long pause, then Philip asked. "Can't you stay a little longer?"

Melissa longed to say "yes", but she couldn't. She was afraid that if she didn't go, their relationship might deteriorate. Philip, after all couldn't be her "tour guide" forever, and what would she do while he was working? If she weren't working, she definitely could not afford Paris.

"We both knew my stay wasn't permanent. I have to go home. This vacation has felt like a dream but, it is time for me to return to my life." She was whispering now.

"What about us? I know you feel something for me, Melissa. What about us?" He repeated.

"We need to talk." She said.

"Yes. I will see you tonight. We can talk then. Unfortunately, I have to go now." He said then he hung up.

"Can't you stay a little longer?" Echoed in her head the rest of the afternoon. Could she stay longer? She had never considered it. But then, she had never intended to meet Philip.

In a perfect world, Philip would have loved her enough to come home with her. "Does he love me enough?" "Does he love me?" Were questions to which she desperately needed answers.

By evening, she had slipped into a slight depression. *Does he love me enough?* Was the question she couldn't answer, yet it kept cycling through her thoughts. Not only was the question plaguing her, but she seemed to have slipped into a fog as well. She tried to watch television, but she couldn't concentrate. She just left it on for the company it provided. At 5:00 PM, she showered and dressed. When she looked at her outfit, she had to laugh! She was wearing two different shoes!

"Get a grip, girl!" She reprimanded herself. "He already told you that Paris was his home now!" She reminded herself. She wondered why people always said: "love conquers all". If Philip wasn't willing to return to America, then their relationship would be long-distance one, a 7,000 mile long- distance one. However, having seen him every day made her realize that seeing him less would be torturous.

She couldn't even consider moving to Paris. It wasn't just the expense, there didn't seem to be any vacancies anyway; and she certainly couldn't live with Philip. Especially since he hadn't asked her to marry him. Even if he did ask her, she couldn't. She would miss her family too much! It was hopeless! Sadly, she realized that there was really no choice to be made. It would be better to end it, than to try to hold on to him with just phone calls and an occasional visit. She would have to return home and learn to live her life without him.

She would go to Nantes with Philip as her good-bye present to herself, then she would fly home and never see him again. Just like she had lost Bill, all those years ago, she would learn to live without Philip. The pain could not last forever, only the memories. If Philip could live without her, then she could live without him! At least that is what she told herself. It would be his choice.

Her phone sounded. Philip was here.

When she exited the hotel, she saw him standing by his car waiting for her. As she approached, he opened the door. As she stepped off the curb, he took her hand and pulled her to himself.

"Melissa." He whispered into her hair as he pulled her into his arms. "I've missed you!" Then he kissed her more passionately than he ever had. She felt like she would faint, except that he was holding her tightly against him.

"Philip, people are watching!" She said, trying to pull away from him.

"Let them watch; I have been waiting all day to kiss you! This is Paris after all." He still hadn't released her. "I can't stop thinking about you!" Finally, he let her get into his car.

"We really need to talk, Philip." She said as seriously as she could. She was trembling from the power of his kiss, but she did her best to speak calmly.

"Yes, we do. I want to take you home with me, but I don't trust myself." He was being honest.

"I understand. I am not sure I can trust myself either." She smiled.

Philip drove around for a while, but he didn't seem to have a destination. Melissa continued to look out of the window.

"I will miss all of this." She said wistfully.

Seeing a parking spot near The Seine, Philip pulled the car over and parked.

"Do you mind if we just walk a while?" He asked.

"No, I don't mind."

As always, he came around to help her out of the car. When he faced her, she saw a hunger in his eyes that she had not seen before. She was glad they had not gone to his apartment. She was not a virgin, but she had not been with a man since her last husband. Having survived a second bad, brief marriage, she had decided that she would probably be celibate the rest of her life. Then Philip had come along. The way he looked at her made her feel naked, beautiful and desirable. His look made feelings that she had long suppressed resurface.

He seemed to need to touch her. He held her hand as they walked, and when they stopped to look at the water, he put his arm around her waist. When they stopped to look at the "Love Locks" section of the bridge, she saw desire in his eyes. Since everyone on the bridge was kissing, he pulled her into his arms to kiss her, and kiss her he did! It was a powerful kiss. It weakened her knees. It caused her heart to pound against his chest. It made her tremble.

"Melissa, Melissa, please don't go!" Philip whispered it again, as he continued to kiss and hold her. "I'm in love with you! I need you!" He spoke into her ear, all the while kissing the life out of her! Had she not been pressed against the bridge, she was sure she would have fainted.

"Oh, Philip, I love you too, but I have to go home. I can't live here. I thought we were going to talk." She reminded him, while pulling away in order to catch her breath and calm herself. "Is there something bad that happened to you that keeps you from coming back?" She asked. Then she continued. "Are you running from the law or something?" She knew he couldn't be, but she just asked in order to get him to explain.

"It isn't that. It's just that in my profession, the work that I do requires that I am here, in Paris. I couldn't do this job in the U.S., and even if I did find a comparable job, I would still have to travel a great deal, and I love living here. It's hard to explain. I am treated like a man, not a Black man. The only thing that matters here is that you embrace being French. I have no family, nor do I have children. My life is here, and has been so for the last 35 years."

"Well, I won't lie and say that things are better at home, but they are different." She continued. "I could put up with anything if you were by my side. Our home would be our sanctuary." She ended.

They walked a while longer, then found themselves near the hospital and the café' where they had eaten when visiting Jean-Rene'. They entered and ordered salads, French bread and wine. They ate silently each one deep in thought.

Melissa was the first to speak. "Have you visited Jean-Rene'?" Melissa asked, knowing that he had, but wanting to change the subject to something other than her impending departure.

"Yes, I see him pretty much every day. I go on my way to the office. He seems to be improving, but I do notice his speech has slowed. I am just so glad he made it!"

"It's getting late. We better go." Melissa suggested.

"I know, but I wish we didn't have to. I can't wait for our trip. Is there anything you need?" He asked.

"Well, I don't have anything in which to swim. I am not really a beach person, but I remember how beautiful the beach was. I didn't think of buying a swimsuit when we were shopping. I'd just as well enjoy walking along the beach. If I change my mind, I am sure we can find a suit when we get there. What time will you be picking me up?"

"What time will you be ready? He asked.

"How about 8:00 am? I can pack some croissants, eggs and bring some coffee from the hotel." Melissa suggested.

"Then I will pick you up at 8:00 am." He drove her back to the hotel. As always, he got out of his car, and though it was only a few feet to the entrance, this time he walked her to the door. Pulling her to himself, he kissed her deeply. "Sleep well, my sweet Melissa." Then he walked back to his car, got in and drove away.

CHAPTER ELEVEN

THE RIDE TO Nantes was both beautiful and wonderful. Seeing the French countryside reminded her that France was really plush and green. She had flown from Paris to Nantes, but never ridden in a car, or on the train. She shared more stories with Philip, telling of her experiences with the family by whom she had been "play-adopted". As always, he hung on her every word; his look was intense. He had the ability to scan her from head to foot. It made her feel exposed, but appreciated, desirable, and admired. She found that she started embellishing her tale in order to keep his eyes on her. His look made her heart race. Luckily, there weren't many cars on the road, or they surely would have had an accident.

"I'm talking so much, Philip!"

"No, I wouldn't say that. If you weren't here, I would probably be listening to a CD or the radio." He said.

"Yes, but you wouldn't be looking at the CD player or the radio while you were driving." She said smiling.

"True." He said smiling back. "Sorry, but any chance I get to look at you, I have to take it." He continued. "With all of the time I have spent in Paris, and traveling with the job, I have never been to Nantes. It is beautiful. I wish we could have more time to tour." Melissa noticed a sadness in his tone.

"I know, but let's not talk about that now." She, too, was sad, but she wanted to enjoy these last days and hours with him. She found that the drive was shorter than she had expected.

"I have booked two rooms. Philip said as they went to the front desk to get their keys. He gave her a key, then picked up her bag. "I really want to spend every minute with you, but I don't think I can trust myself to be in the same room especially at night. The night I spent on the couch when Jean-Rene' was ill, was torturous, knowing that you were so close! I had trouble falling to sleep, and my dreams were about you!"

"Oh, Philip. You say the most wonderful things to me!" Melissa replied, her voice a whisper.

"That's because you are wonderful. I have never felt like this about any woman. I thought my job fulfilled me, until I met you." Philip said. Melissa smiled.

"I'm so excited to be here. What should be do first? Tour or eat?" She asked in order to change the subject.

"Let's change and meet in the lobby in say, 20 minutes?" He suggested.

"Great! We can eat lunch and make our plans then."

Philip took her bag and her key. He walked her to her room; opened her door, then walked in and placed her bag on the bed.

"This is really nice, Philip. Thanks for booking this room."

"It is my pleasure." He turned from the bed and stood looking down at her, then without warning he pulled her to him. He buried his face in her neck and planted a kiss there. Melissa felt a shiver of desire flow through her.

"Melissa, don't go back. Don't leave me. I need you so much." He whispered in her hair. Melissa was stunned! She had wanted him to kiss her and hold her, but the way he was holding her made her tremble. He hadn't ever really held her that tightly. She placed her hands on his chest and felt his heart pounding. Then she slid her hands up around his neck to return his kiss; and though it was supposed to be a light kiss, it turned out to be something more, deeper and hungrier.

"I don't know if I can make it without you!" He whispered. "All the time that I have spent here in France, I have been a workaholic. I've had no social life, and no women in my life. I just worked and went home to complete work that I hadn't finished. Rumors had it that something was wrong with me, because I didn't seem to be interested in women, but trust me, I had many opportunities to prove people wrong. I was trying to honor my mother, and my faith. I knew that one day I would marry, so I vowed to wait." He continued. "I also promised myself that I would never become my father. 'He never met a woman he didn't like.' He destroyed our home and my mother with his cheating. Then I met you! I'm in torment! I want you so badly! I feel like I am losing my mind! You are in my every thought. I feel like I'll go crazy if I can't be with you! You can't do this to me, and then leave me! I love you more than I ever imagined it was possible to love someone!"

Melissa was stunned! This handsome, beautiful, intelligent man was saying he had never been with a woman!! She would be his first lover, if she gave in to his kisses!! It was frightening but so sweet. He was a virgin, she wasn't. Though briefly and badly, she had been married twice, and had never really enjoyed her husbands, because they were like his father, cheaters. They never seemed to care about her. That he would share this intimate fact with her, touched her! But, it also told her that she couldn't love him, then leave him.

"Oh Philip, I don't know what to say."

"Do you love me, Melissa?"

"Yes, Philip. I do, but love isn't always enough." She said sadly then she moved away from him and sat on the bed. He joined her, then reached for her hand.

"What are we going to do? I can't leave Paris, and you won't stay." He commented.

"Let's not spoil our time here. Let's enjoy Nantes. We need to think this through. Come on, let's make this a weekend to remember!" She stood up and pulled Philip up. But when she did so, he was again facing her, and he pulled her close.

"One more for the road." He said, encircling her in his arms and kissing her senseless! When he finished, she took several deep breaths to steady herself. Her heart was beating so fast, that she thought she might faint.

"Are you okay?" Philip was smiling. It made him feel good to see how his kisses affected her.

A few doors down from their hotel, they found a small café and ordered bread, cheese, salad and soda. Philip sat across from her, watching her every move. His look was so intense that she had a difficult time swallowing. To break the tension, she told him about the German bunker that the family had taken her to see. He said that there wasn't enough time to see it; but, if they came again; they would make a point of visiting it.

When Philip said, "next time", Melissa drew in a breath. Would there be a "next time"? She wondered.

"Yes, next time." She said, then she tried to smile. Not wanting to talk about "next time"; she continued telling Philip about the bunker on the beach. Though she couldn't remember where it was exactly, she knew that the beach at Normandy was less than a day's drive, but not close.

"The bunkers were left by the Germans in World War II. She continued. "If you have every watched "Saving Private Ryan", you get to see how the Germans basically slaughtered the American soldiers as they tried to storm the beach. It is a difficult scene to watch, but I force myself to watch the movie during Memorial Day, just for my father. He was a World War II Veteran, but he never talked about the war with the thin helmets, non-insulated clothing, lack of appropriate medication and such...." Melissa's voice softened to almost a whisper as she continued to think of her father, then she seemed to shake off her sadness. "I guess that's why my father drank. He never talked about it. If I hadn't loved my father, growing up would have been really tough. He drank almost every weekend. We never had more than "just enough"; yet, he seldom missed a day of work. He didn't hit us, but he would yell and scream. We always had a neighbor who would take us in until "the storm was over". Then, on Sundays he would drink a gallon of milk to, as he put it, "clean out his system", so he would be ready for work on Mondays." She continued. "I am sure he had PTSD, but the family just called him 'that old drunk'. After he died, my sister sent me a paper she had found that showed that he had been a decorated war hero." She continued. "Funny, but he never drank when he was unemployed." She smiled sadly.

"It sounds like you had a good father except for the drinking. Philip reached over to hold her hand. He desperately wanted to help her get over the sadness that had taken her over. He stood up and came to sit next to her. He put his arms around her, and kissed her. Luckily, there weren't many people in the café. He really didn't care.

"Only God knows how much I want to hold you right now!" Philip whispered in her ear. His breath on her ear made her shiver. "Are you cold." He asked, concerned.

"No. It's just when you hold me, my body responds in ways it hasn't in a very long time. It amazes me how much you affect me." Philip smiled broadly, and her heart stopped! He was the most beautiful man she had ever known, inside and out!

"I wish I had known you when we were little. Look how much more time we would have had together." He paused. "Let's go take a walk and see what we can before dark."

"Yes, let's."

They found Nantes to be like Paris, only smaller, less cosmopolitan, and less modern. It was walking back into time.

"I remember that there was a beautiful mall with all kinds of shops here. Walking through it was like walking through a castle; and there really is a castle here too. She explained.

"Well, let's walk until we find both." Philip responded.

By evening, they had found the two sites, so they decided to find a place to eat. To their surprise, they found a restaurant that looked like a McDonalds; however, instead of advertising hamburgers, it was advertising "American French Fries".

"That's the first time I have ever seen a restaurant like that. You can order fries with a side of a hamburger!" She commented.

For the first time since she had met him, he laughed hard. In fact, he laughed so hard that she started laughing too. They stood outside of the restaurant holding each other, and laughing until tears formed in Melissa's eyes.

It must have been the tension from the last several weeks that made them laugh, finally they found a bench near the restaurant where they could sit and compose themselves.

"Do you think we dare go in, after laughing so hard out front?" Philip chuckled as he spoke. "Why don't you go in and order for the both of us, and I will hold this bench, so we can eat here." Philip suggested. "They saw me laughing, but they only saw your back." He continued.

"Okay, so do you want the 'hamburger on the side'! With that she started giggling again.

"And a coke!" He added, while laughing softly.

So, Melissa went in and placed two orders. She dared not look out of the window to see what Philip was doing. She knew that if she made "eye contact" with him, she would start laughing again, and she didn't want to drop the food, or make a spectacle of herself.

After paying for their order, she walked to the door and put her back to it in order to return outside to Philip. He had composed himself so he got up and helped her with the food. Then they returned to their bench to eat.

"I've never heard you laugh before, Philip." Melissa said softly.

"I haven't done it much, but you bring me more joy and

happiness than I've known before." He wanted to ask her to stay again, but he thought it would ruin their mood, so they both ate in silence. When they were done, it was getting dark and the city lights were coming on.

Melissa was first to break the silence. "I hope you remember how to get back to the hotel, because I have no idea where we are." She said to Philip as he stood up.

"Well, I haven't paid attention either, and I thought maybe you would remember. The only thing that I have been paying attention to is you." He said, smiling down at her.

"Well, we are in trouble now!" She teased. "Let's Google it!" Melissa smiled.

After getting directions, they walked hand-in-hand back to the hotel.

Again, Philip walked Melissa to her room, took her key and unlocked the door. He went in first and turned on her light.

"All clear." He said softly and smiled. "Thank you for a wonderful day!"

"It was good to hear you laugh, Philip." She told him.

"You too." He said as he approached her.

"Shall we go to the beach tomorrow?" He asked.

"If you want to; although I'm not the greatest of swimmers, and I haven't yet purchased a swimsuit." She answered.

"Good night then." Philip said as he bent down and kissed her forehead, then he left.

Melissa stood in the middle of the floor feeling abandoned. She wondered why he hadn't really kissed her. He always seemed to enjoy kissing her. Had she done something wrong? She wondered. Confused and a little sad, she changed clothes into her gown and just before she got in bed, she heard a light knock on her door.

She looked through the peep hole and saw Philip standing there. When she opened the door, he stepped in and in the same moment took her into his arms.

"I just wanted to give you time to put your gown on." He was smiling, but the look in his eye held no smile. "I came back for my goodnight kiss." With that he kissed her until they were both breathless. Then he released her, and left!

CHAPTER TWELVE

MELISSA STOOD IN the middle of the room feeling helpless. Was he trying to torture her? How could he do that to her? She was tempted to go to his room and get back at him. She knew he was teasing her, or maybe "torturing" was the more appropriate word, or perhaps he was trying to tempt her! Whatever he was doing, she knew it was an attempt to make her stay.

She slipped in between the covers and before she realized it, she was crying. What was she going to do? How could she leave him, just get on the plane and fly away? He owned her heart, he owned her soul, and even though they hadn't been intimate; he owned her body.

Things were different the next day. They were pleasant to each other, but they did everything in their power to not touch. No hand holding, no kissing, no looking into each other's eyes. They had passed "the point of no return", and one of them would have to make a major decision if they were going to be together.

At breakfast, Philip spoke first. "I don't think it would be a good idea to go to the beach at all. I couldn't bear to see you in a bathing suit, and not be able to make love to you. I don't know how much more torture I can stand!" He said it as if he were exhausted.

"I understand, Philip, and I am sorry!" She responded.

"Maybe we should just head back so we can figure out what we are going to do." He said.

"Yes, maybe we should." She agreed.
"How long will it take you to pack?"
"I can be ready in half an hour."
"Then, I will meet you in the lobby." He stood, then pulled her chair out for her.

Their joyful, hopeful weekend had somehow turned sour. The decision that one of them would have to make weighed heavily on them both.

The return ride was quiet. What had started off as an exciting weekend now seemed to make them feel like they had attended a funeral. They rode the rest of the way in silence. From time to time Philip would look over at her, but he didn't speak. His face was like a mask, except for his jaw which was pulsing.

Philip desired Melissa like no other woman he had ever known. He had come to the point that her kisses were no longer enough. He knew that he wasn't a "saint"'; and even had he been Catholic, he would never have taken a vow of celibacy.

He had felt that at his age, perhaps his didn't have the feelings that most men had until he had met Melissa. His desire for her was more powerful than anything that he had ever experienced! She occupied his thoughts constantly! Cold showers weren't doing him much good anymore! But, the thought of not seeing her, not holding or kissing her, was unbearable!

He continued to think about the day that would come when she had to go home. He vowed to stop seeing her in order to save himself from the torture, but he couldn't. He loved her! He loved her! Whatever she decided, he would consent. He loved her!

Just outside of Paris, it started to rain. It seemed that even the skies were saddened about their situation. When Philip pulled up in front of Melissa's hotel, as always, he got out to open the door for her. They stood facing each other as the rain increased. She was glad that it was raining. She could let her tears flow and only Philip could see them.

Philip's eyes were intense. She felt like he could see her soul. "I know you love me." He said. "Why won't you stay a little longer?" He asked her again.

"I have to go home, Philip." Her voice was a whisper.

"No matter how much you love me? I see it in your eyes. I feel it when you kiss me..." He pulled her into his arms for one final kiss, a kiss she would never forget, because she knew it would be her last.

They stood in the rain holding each other. Then he broke away to take her case into the lobby. She turned to follow him, but her feet wouldn't move. She just stood in the rain waiting. When he returned, she was drenched, but still standing where he had left her. He faced her one last time. Melissa leaned into him, pressing her cheek to his breast. She felt his heart racing.

"Philip...I...;" was all she managed to say. Her throat was dry, and she suddenly had a headache.

He was the first to break the silence. "I don't think I can see you off. I think we should say our "good-byes" now. "I love you, Melissa, but I can't do this. If you are going to leave me, then I think a clean break is best."

"I understand, Philip. I do. In my heart, I know that you are right, it's just that not seeing you again..." Her voice trailed off. She couldn't think. The lump in her throat felt like it was the size of an apple.

As he walked to the driver's side of his car, all she could say was "Philip, I...." Her voice was a whisper. Both her head and heart were pounding so hard that she felt like she was going to faint! She took one step toward the hotel, then turned back. He was instantly there his arms around her to steady her. She leaned into him, not wanting to say "good-bye".

She felt like her heart was going to either explode or stop beating! They stood facing each other. Melissa wrapped her arms around his waist.

"Stay." Philip whispered in her ear. She felt his breath and the soft caress of his lips. It sent waves of desire throughout her body.

"I can't." She could barely get the words out.

"Then goodbye, my love." With that, Philip took her arms from around his waist, walked back to his car, got in and drove away.

CHAPTER THIRTEEN

THE NEXT DAY, Melissa felt numb. She didn't want to get out of bed, but she knew that she must. The concierge came up and knocked on her door to see if she needed help packing. When she saw Melissa, she expressed her concern.

"Oh, là!" You come down and have breakfast. Is your gentleman friend coming today?" She asked.

Melissa didn't know what to say; so, she lied and told her that he had to go out of town on business. She knew that the woman didn't believe her, but she smiled and tried again to encourage Melissa go to breakfast.

"I have to pack. My flight is this afternoon." Melissa informed her.

"I hope you will come back again and stay with us. It has been a pleasure having you here, and your French is very good." The concierge said.

"Merci beaucoup." Melissa responded. She tried to smile, but couldn't.

"If you need help with your bags or anything please let me know."

Melissa packed everything she had brought. When it came to the casual clothes that Philip had brought for their weekend, she sat down on the bed hugged herself and cried. She cried quietly, but when she finished, her chest hurt, and her eyes were swollen and red.

At Noon, she asked the concierge to call her a taxi. A man was sent up to help her carry her bags downstairs to the lobby. When the taxi arrived she hugged the concierge, said "adieu" (good-bye) and got in. When she entered the taxi, she took one last look at the hotel. The concierge waved from the doorway and reminded her that it was not "adieu" (good-bye), but "au revoir" (see you again). Melissa smiled, but said nothing. She didn't think she could or would ever return to Paris. The trip that had started off so wonderfully, had ended painfully.

She was glad that she hadn't taken many pictures because every picture would remind her of Philip. She felt like she was losing her mind! She knew that she loved him, because she felt like she was going to die, that any minute her heart was going to explode, or just stop beating.

At the airport she looked for Philip, hoping he would change his mind and come so that she could see him one last time, but he didn't. When the plane taxied down the runway, it took everything within her to keep from calling the stewardess to have the flight stopped. So, she bowed her head and sobbed silently. It was a blessing that she was by the window. She turned away from the passengers sitting beside her so no one could see her tears. Mercifully, she cried herself to sleep.

The flight was uneventful. When she deplaned, she saw her grandchildren, and her youngest son whose name was also "Philip". She was grateful that his nickname was "Phil", because she didn't think she could say "Philip" without crying. Putting on a brave front, she smiled and hugged them all.

"Did you have a good time, grandma? We missed you so much!" Her grandchildren spoke in unison. Melissa smiled.

Phil, informed her that her oldest son, Joseph, couldn't take off from work, but he would talk to her that evening.

"Mom, you look tired. Are you okay?" Her son asked.

"Yes, I'm fine. I think that I tried to do too much. After I rest, I'll be my old self." She told him. But, in her heart, she knew that it would take a long time until she was, if ever.

They drove her home, and said good-bye. "Will you be keeping the kids next week, or do you want me to take some more time off?" Phil asked.

"I'm fine. I am going straight to bed. The way I feel, I will probably stay there all weekend but, I will be at your place bright and early, Monday morning."

"Thanks Mom. It's so good to have you back!" She gave them each another hug after they helped her carry her suitcases into her house. Then she handed out the gifts that she had bought them.

She didn't bother to unpack. She didn't have the strength, so she just went to her couch and laid down. She slept until morning. She was so emotionally exhausted that she realized that she hadn't dreamed at all, and she felt that that was a small blessing.

That afternoon, she carried her suitcases upstairs and started to unpack her clothes. She found that each outfit had a memory. She felt incredibly sad, but she didn't cry; however, when she started unpacking her souvenirs the tears returned, and when she unwrapped the picture of Napoleon that Philip had bought her, she had to hug her pillow to quiet the sobs that wracked her body. She cried until she fell asleep. He was in her dream. He was calling to her, and reaching for her. When she woke up, she was exhausted. Even so, she busied herself by putting things away, and washing and putting away her clothes.

In the evening, she fixed herself something to eat, then went to bed early. All she wanted to do was sleep. It was only in her dreams that she could be with Philip. But, she knew she had to forget about him and resume her life. On Monday morning, she resumed her grandmother duties and went to her son's house to take the kids to school.

After taxiing her granddaughters to and from school, and watching her little grandson, for a week, she thought she was feeling better, but a long way from "back to normal". Phil asked to talk to her on Friday evening. When she entered his home, she was happy to see that her oldest son had come as well. She hugged him and then sat down facing them both.

"Mom, what's wrong?" Joseph asked.

"Nothing. Why do you ask?" Melissa responded.

"You just haven't been yourself since you came home. Both Phil and I are concerned." Joseph explained.

"I haven't?"

"No, mom, you haven't. You seem to be doing things like you always do, but your mind is somewhere else. What happened in Paris?"

"I know this may sound unbelievable to you both, but I met someone, and I fell in love." She explained to them.

"I think that's great, but why are you so sad." They both asked

"He lives in Paris, and doesn't want to return here. He says that he has built his life there."

"What are you going to do?" They asked.

"I guess I will have to forget him. He is a wonderful man. I wish that you could meet him. If he truly cares about me, perhaps he will come for a visit and you can."

"My Mom is in love! S-W-E-E-T!" Phil said and hugged her.

"I am sure it will work out." Joseph said. Then he added. "Have a little faith, Mom." He got up and came to sit next to her on the couch to hug her. "What's this guy's name anyway?"

"His name is Philip, too. Philip Nance." At the mention of his name her eyes filled with tears. She had not spoken it since returning home. Joseph reached in his pocket and handed her a handkerchief.

"Sorry, Mom! I didn't mean to make you cry!" He said while awkwardly patting her on her back. "You really liked this dude, huh? Why didn't you stay longer?" He asked.

"Because I love you two, and my grandchildren, and I want to be here with you all, at least until they are older." She said while wiping her eyes.

"Maybe this dude will have a change of heart, and move back here." Phil suggested.

"Or, perhaps someday he will visit and you can all meet him."

"Cool. I hope so." Phil said, and Joseph agreed.

When she thought about Philip meeting her family, she smiled to herself. If only he would come! That thought carried her through most days, but her heart ached. She began to busy herself more in order to put him out of her mind. She dug out her old sewing machine and made clothes for her grandchildren, she took Zumba Classes at the YMCA, she took classes at the junior college, she took up gardening and she continued to be the taxi for her granddaughters and a sitter for the baby boy. Whatever she could do to keep her mind off Philip, she did. But, nothing really helped!

After about 6 months had passed, she realized that she could think about Philip without bursting into tears. She loved him, she dreamed about him, but she was learning to live without him. Christmas was coming, and she busied herself with plans for parties, gifts, etc.

On Christmas Eve, after she decorated her tree, she placed her family gifts under it. It was traditional for her to spend the night with her family. So, she packed her night clothes and went to join them.

She knew her sons to be "last minute" shoppers, so when she got to Phil's house, she didn't mind not seeing anything with her name on it under his tree. Her sons usually pitched in together to get her something expensive and wonderful, so she knew she wouldn't be disappointed with their gift; however, she thought that they were really cutting it close this year!

Christmas morning, still no gift! She was disappointed, but

she didn't say anything. After everyone had opened theirs, her sons hugged her and explained that her gift was not there yet, but it would be coming by special delivery later that day.

"Well, since it is Christmas Day, can't you tell me what it is?" She asked.

"Nope! We don't want to spoil the surprise," was all her sons said.

Just as they were about to sit down to dinner, the doorbell rang.

"That must be your gift." Her sons said in unison. "Why don't you get the door, Mom."

"Sure thing." Melissa was so excited!

She took off her apron, and went to the door. There was no one there, but there was a small box on the door step with a note attached to it and a bouquet of flowers.

She picked up the box and the flowers, and returned to the dinner table.

"We hope you like it." They all said. She laid the flowers on the dining room table, and returned to the living room with the small box in her hand.

"Open it Grandma!" Sang the kids.

With her hands shaking, she untied the ribbon and opened the box. A beautiful and expensive diamond ring was inside. She quizzically looked at her sons. "You bought me a ring?"

Her sons said chuckling. "No, Mom, read the card." They each said.

She opened the card and read it. "I am here my love, come to me." There was an address and room number to a hotel at the bottom of the note. It was signed "Philip".

"Do you like our gift?" Her sons were beaming and spoke simultaneously.

"What did you two do?" Melissa whispered.

"We tracked him down, and told him that if he didn't come visit you, one of us would fly over there to Paris and kick his butt!"

"Oh, you didn't!"

"Oh yes we did!"

"Nobody's going to break my mother's heart while I'm alive! Commented Phil.

"True that!" Echoed Joseph.

"What are you waiting for? Go!" Joseph added while getting her coat.

"You don't have to ask me twice!!" Melissa was beyond excited! Philip had come!

"Save us some food, I will bring him back so you all can meet him." With that, she put on her coat and hat and flew out of the door.

She dove to the hotel address on the card. Luckily, there was a valet service because she would have left the car in the middle of the street! She flew into the lobby and ran to the elevators. She got off the elevator and ran down the hallway until she found his door. Gathering her breath, she knocked. There was no "who is it." The door just opened, and there was Philip. He was dressed like he had dressed the first day she had met him; gray tie, gray suit, gray shoes and white shirt. He looked so good!

"Philip." That was all she was allowed to say before he pulled her into the room and then into his arms. His kiss was indescribable!

"Yes, my love?" He answered after a long passionate kiss.

"You came! I thought I would die, but you came. Are you going back?" She asked timidly.

"Maybe for a visit now and then, Jean-Rene' has passed. I have fully retired and the business has been sold. So, since I am unemployed and can't live without you, I guess I have to stay." He said nuzzling her neck. "Did you get the ring?" He asked.

"Yes, it's beautiful!"

"Then, will you be my wife?" He asked as he knelt on one knee.

"Yes! Yes! A million times yes!!!

Then he sat down with her on the bed and placed the ring on her finger. He turned to the house phone. "I need a minister to come to Room 777. If you don't send one soon, someone is going to die!" He said into the receiver. "That ought to get someone up here "toute de suite" (immediately)." He smiled as he returned to sit with Melissa on the bed.

In about 5 minutes, there was a frantic knock on the door. Philip got up and opened it. The concierge ran in with an EMT crew and a minister. "Where's the person who is ill?" He shouted frantically.

"It's me!" Philip said.

"I don't understand." Said the concierge with a confused look on his face.

"Is this the minister?" Philip asked.

"Yes." The concierge said.

"Good." Philip said, then he went to Melissa and sat next to her on the bed again.

"If you don't marry us right now, I am going to die!" He was smiling at her.

Breathing a sigh of relief, the concierge suggested they go down to one of the small dining rooms off of the lobby were the décor would be much better. As they prepared to do so, the elevator opened and her sons and grandchildren stepped out.

"Did you know about this?" She asked her sons.

"Know about it, we planned it!" They said, while grinning from ear to ear.

"Oh, boys. I knew you were good sons, but this is something I will never forget. So, you have obviously met Philip, and you like him?" She asked.

"He's a good man, Momma. I am so happy for you!" Her son Phil said. Then both of her sons turned to Philip.

"But", Joseph added, "if you ever hurt my Mom again, me and you are going to settle it like men! You get my drift?" He said seriously.

"Bien sur, I mean, got it!" Philip responded. Then turning to Melissa, he added "Your sons are also good men!"

Luckily, Melissa had dressed for dinner but regrettably she was not dressed for a wedding. However, she didn't care, she was so happy. She would have married Philip wearing a garbage bag!

"Allons-y!" Philip said, while linking his arm through Melissa's and walking to the elevator.

The ceremony was beautiful, but short. The grandchildren had brought flowers and chocolates. They returned to her son Philip's house to have dinner, which he had arranged to be catered.

"I guess I will have to take a week off so you two can have a honeymoon." Phil suggested. But both Melissa and Philip disagreed.

"We don't need a honeymoon!" They said in unison, then smiled at each other.

Then Melissa explained. "We met in Paris. We fell in love in Paris. Now, we can honeymoon here in our home."

"Our home." Philip repeated softly while reaching for her hand.

"We can take a hint!" Joseph said as he winked at her. She tried not to blush, but she couldn't help but notice the gleam in Philip's eyes. Philip her husband, and soon to be her lover. She couldn't wait!

Melissa stood. "Beloved sons of mine, if you don't mind; I am sure Philip is tired from his trip, and I want to show him his new home, so we will be spending the rest of Christmas at my place, our place." She corrected herself, as she smiled and grabbed Philip's hand.

Phil added. "Please come over tomorrow morning for breakfast.

Then Philip turned to Melissa. "Is your home far from here?"

"Actually, no. Phil and I are neighbors." Melissa smiled, then continued. "I bought my house next door so I could be available whenever he needed a sitter, although sometimes Joseph helps out too. She explained.

"Then we will to see you in the morning, say around 10:00 am?" Joseph asked.

With that Melissa hugged her grandchildren and sons as Philip shook hands then helped Melissa put on her coat. Then he picked up his suitcase.

"Thank you for all you have done to bring us back together. I owe you a great deal." He said to her sons.

"No problem. Just be good to our Mom. That's all we ask." Phil, said as Joseph nodded in agreement.

"You have my word." Philip responded.

Melissa and Philip walked next door. Once inside Melissa's home she noticed that Philip seemed nervous. She thought that was sweet!

"Are you okay?" She asked. "You must be tired from the stress of moving here. Do you want to unpack or shall we just go to bed?"

Immediately, Philip pulled her to himself. "I want to go to bed, but not to sleep!" He said. He was smiling and his dark eyes were brighter than she had ever seen them. Then he whispered in her ear. "Be gentle with me. This is my first time!"

His breath on her ear sent shivers through her body. "I make no promises!" Melissa said, as she took his hand. "Let me show you how much I love you!" She added as she turned off the lights and led him upstairs to their bedroom.

"Oh, là!" Philip whispered as he followed her.

The End